Saving Twigs

Charles Tabb

DEDICATION

For Brooke. You left us far too soon.

ACKNOWLEDGMENTS AND THANKS

No work of fiction is ever truly written alone. Many people are a part of the creation. Heartfelt thanks are hereby extended to my Beta readers, Sue Schorling, Chuck Shelton, Trisha Shelton, Elin Call, and my wife, Dee, my best critic. Your fearless critiques make my work so much better than I ever could have done on my own. Thank you to my editor, the wonderful Kristine Elder. You're amazing! A tremendous thank you also goes out to those who have encouraged me throughout the process of writing my books and stories especially members of the Hanover Writers Club and Harry Heckel, a gifted author whose occasional lunches with me keep me sane. A loving thank you to my brothers, Bill and George. You remind me how proud our mother would be.

Finally, thank you, dear reader, for reading this book. As authors, we scatter our words into the wind, hoping someone appreciates them. I am so happy that you appreciate them enough to read my humble offerings.

It's said that the love of money is the root of all evil, but selfishness is the root of all sin.

—Anonymous

Non nobis solum nati sumus. (Not for ourselves alone are we born.)

—Marcus Tullius Cicero

What you did for the least of these, you did for me.

—Jesus of Nazareth

1

I love walks, especially on warm, breezy days like today when the sun is so bright it's blinding even when you don't look right at it. My mama says the sun gave me my red hair. She says one day the sun just reached right down and touched it and it turned into the flaming red it is now. I used to believe her, but I'm too old for that now.

Anyway, I'm on a walk right now to think about things, especially the events from three years ago. I imagine I will be taking a lot of these walks to figure it all out and get perspective, as my mom would say. I need perspective because it might be the only thing that will keep me sane after all that has happened. What I'm telling you will start out light, like any thirteen-year-old girl's life, but I have to warn you—it gets pretty heavy later on.

I guess I should tell you a little about myself before I get into all the stuff that brought me to this point. I'm sixteen now, but what I'm going to tell you about happened back when I was thirteen. Funny how it seems like yesterday but it doesn't. Time plays a lot of tricks on us. At least, that's what my Mom says. Three years ago seems like forever, but it also seems like last week. Like I said, it's funny how time is like that. Mom says it gets worse as I grow older. Great. Another thing not to look forward to.

My name is Maureen Lindstrom. I'll go ahead and tell you I hate that name. It's not that I hate the name Maureen. It's just that I never met anyone else my age with that name because it sounds old-fashioned, but my Mom insisted on naming me after her grandmother. Besides, I had that red mop of hair that reminded my mom of this actress from years ago named Maureen O'Hara. I'd go by my middle name with people my age, but that one is even worse: Dickson. Sorry, no thanks. It's not even a name, or at least not a first name, and even if it was, I wouldn't use it. I don't think I have to say why. Anyway, my mom insisted on giving me my dad's middle name. So back on July 27, 2003, I was born in Pensacola, Florida, where my mom lived at the time, and given two names I would hate forever. Yeah, lucky me.

I never actually met my dad. He was a cop who was killed when he went to a domestic disturbance call before I was born. He knocked on the door and the guy inside opened the door holding a gun and shot my dad before he had a chance to say anything. At least that's what my mom said happened. My dad's partner shot the guy who killed my dad. I'm not sure how I feel about that, really. I mean, I know he was my dad and all, but I also never met him. It's weird.

My mom married my dad when they were both twenty-one. Her name is Brandy Marie (another reason for "Maureen") Shaw Lindstrom. She owns a local nursery and flower shop. She says she got interested in plants working for a lady when she was a teenager after she got in some trouble and managed to be found innocent of the crime.

Since I know you're going to be curious about that, I'll tell you that she ran over a guy who had more or less taken her prisoner. She ran off with the guy when she was all confused about things in her life at the time. I asked her if she killed him on purpose, and she says she doesn't know because she doesn't actually remember doing it. I asked if she was drunk or high on something, but she says she wasn't. Just scared. He was robbing this place in Jacksonville, Florida, and she was supposed to drive getaway. She'd only driven a car a couple of times before, and she was in a terrible life with this creep. He actually would lock her in the small apartment they shared and be gone all day. He would steal cars and sell them for a living. Yeah, I know. A real prince.

I asked her the guy's name, but she wouldn't tell me. She said he didn't deserve a name. I can't say as I blame her.

Now, we live in Denton, Florida, where my grandma moved to when my mom was my age now. Grandma moved them all to Florida so she could marry a man she ended up divorcing a few years later.

My Uncle Ryan is in the Air Force, stationed at Ramstein Air Base in Germany. I think he's lucky. He's nice to me whenever we see him, which isn't much. He hasn't visited in two years. He's married and has twin sons two years older than me and a daughter who's twelve. I like Uncle Ryan's wife, but I barely know my cousins since I've only seen them about six or seven times in my life.

Anyway, I guess that's enough about me. You'll learn more about me as I tell you my story.

Like I said, though, what I'm going to tell you about happened three years ago. I was only thirteen and sort of lonely for friends. I mean, I had friends, but I was getting sort of tired of the ones I had. None of them were like besties or anything, and I guess I wanted someone like that.

The weird part was the bestie I ended up meeting was a guy. I know that may not sound all that weird, but it felt like it, especially at the time. A thirteen-year-old girl has a lot of stuff she needs to talk about, some of it kind of private, so I was needing another girl to talk to about life and relationships, but it turned out to be a guy instead. As it turned out, maybe he needed a bestie more than I did.

Anyway, it all started when I had just turned thirteen. My body was changing and life seems to sort of rush itself along when that starts happening, like there's this race to see how fast childhood can crumble into dust. I know I was wanting things to slow down a bit, but of course, that wasn't happening. As my mom said, you can't stop nature from moving at its own pace.

I remember it was right after my grandmother moved in with us. I know a lot of girls get along with their grandmothers like bees and honey, but that's not the way it is with me. Grandma and I butted heads like crazy. It seemed like everything I wanted to do she didn't like.

Wear makeup? You're too young.

Wear ragged blue jeans? You're too pretty.

Go on dates? You're too gullible.

I had to look that one up on my phone, and its meaning made me mad. Did she think I was stupid or something?

Anyway, it was like that all the time, and the worst part was my mom took her side. Every. Single. Time.

I called a girl named Cameron that I knew from my science class to complain, but she was like, we all have to deal with that. Well, that wasn't what I wanted to hear, so I decided I needed a real bestie who would get mad about it like me.

One thing I had to be careful with was picking the wrong person to tell my secrets to. I liked Cameron, but she could be judgmental sometimes. She wasn't cruel about it. She just sometimes acted like what you did was worse than you even thought it was.

Then, as if my wish was being granted by some fairy godmother or something, the very next day in school, I met Nick.

Nick's family had just moved to Denton, and that was his first day at our school. He was put at the table in science class that I shared with two other girls, my friend Cameron and Mia, who was so boy crazy she made me want to apologize for the rest of the girls in the world.

Don't get me wrong. I like boys and did back then, too, but I've never been out of my mind over some guy. That's probably because of what happened to my mom when she was a teenager, and she described herself as a lot like Mia. My mom raised me to believe no guy is worth losing my mind over, no matter how much being around him made me feel, as she put it, "all melty."

"There are plenty of nice guys out there, like your dad. You just have to do a lot of searching to find one good enough to devote yourself to," she'd told me about a thousand times. Anyway, I guess her words stuck.

Mia, on the other hand, was like my mom when she was a teenager. Some guy would walk by her, and she'd roll her eyes with what can only be described as a "wanting." I thought it was the picture of insanity.

Cameron was sort of like me, except she wasn't real bestie material for me, like I said.

So, needless to say, when Nick was introduced to the class as a new student from Michigan, Mia looked like she was about to start drooling. Cameron looked at me and just shrugged at Mia's obvious flirting the second Nick sat down, as if to say, *we all have to deal with that*.

I suppose Nick was good-looking with his shock of dark brown hair that flipped across his forehead and shy smile, but I was not really attracted to him. I wasn't even thinking of him becoming a bestie candidate. He just seemed like a nice guy.

One thing was he barely said three words that first class. A lot of guys would try to talk up Mia at least, given her obvious attraction reaction. Nick just sort of stayed to himself.

At lunch that day, Mia was going on about how

6

lucky it was that Mr. Clay seated Nick at our table.

"Mia, we had the only empty seat in the class," I reminded her, but her response remained focus on the luck.

"I know! Wasn't that lucky?!"

I spied Nick sitting at a lunch table by himself the next day and invited him to join us. I would have sat alone with him, but first, that would start rumors flying like rolls in a food fight, and second, Mia would have hated me forever because she would think I was after Nick for myself.

"Hey," I said after approaching the otherwise empty table where he sat. "Want to come sit with us?"

He looked puzzled, like I was asking him the answer to a particularly difficult math problem. Then I guess he recognized me and said, "Sure." No smile. No look of gratitude. Nothing. Just "sure."

He followed me to where Mia was drooling and Cameron was whispering to Mia, probably trying to get her to tone it down a bit.

As he sat, Mia said, "Hey! What part of Michigan are you from?" as if she knew the state's geography.

"Grand Rapids."

"Cool!" Mia gushed. "Is that near Detroit?"

"Not really. It's on the other side of the state, not that far from Lake Michigan."

Any fool could tell he wasn't interested in Mia the way she was interested in him. Okay, nobody could be interested in anyone quite the way Mia was interested in Nick, but what I'm saying is he didn't seem much interested in any kind of teenage romance. She, of course, hadn't noticed his lack of interest at all.

"So, tell us about Grand Rapids!" Mia continued. "Tell us about your friends there. What are they like?"

Mia was obviously fishing for info on a possible love interest he left behind, but he wasn't cooperating.

He shrugged. "Not much to tell."

"Well, you had friends, didn't you?" Cameron asked, obviously ready to feel bad for him if he was friendless in Michigan.

"Yeah. I just don't like to talk about people when they're not around."

Okay, this was different. Most kids our age would rather talk about other people than go to a movie, which was a big reason we liked to gather together at places like movie theaters in the first place.

I think this was my first inkling that he might be bestie material. He apparently had no interest in blabbing secrets, even to people who didn't know the people whose secrets he would be blabbing.

I said, "You'd make a great spy."

That was the first time he really smiled at me. It wasn't a flirty smile, just a nice one. He seemed to appreciate the compliment.

When I looked over at Mia, she was looking daggers at me.

The conversation went on like that until we had to go to our next class. Mostly Mia asking questions and Nick doing his best to say as little as possible.

My next class was English with Ms.

Henderson, so we all parted to go our separate ways, or at least I thought we did. Nick asked where Ms. Henderson's room was. I glanced at Mia before answering. I knew she wouldn't like this, but what was I going to do? Be rude and not tell him I was headed there myself?

"I'm going there myself," I said.

"Great," he answered, and we walked past a fuming Mia toward our next class.

As it happened, my fairy godmother was at work again without my knowing it since the seat in the row next to where I sat was empty, and Ms. Henderson allowed us to choose where we sat. Our choice, though, wasn't a "change your seat every day" thing. Once we made a choice, that was our seat unless she moved us or we asked permission to move.

As we entered the room, I said, "The seat next to mine is open if you want to sit there."

"Won't the teacher tell me where to sit?" he asked.

I explained Ms. Henderson's "choose your own seat" policy.

He shrugged, as if he couldn't care less where he sat and took the empty seat in the row next to where I sat.

He began readying himself for class, so I did the same. After the bell rang and Ms. Henderson asked Nick to introduce himself, which he did as quickly as possible—"Hi, I'm Nick"—I began to wonder why I wasn't falling for him the way Mia was. I could tell from the glances of some of the other girls in class that he was definitely considered a prize, but I had no interest in that at all. In fact, if he'd asked me out on a date, I would have gladly informed him that my mother wouldn't allow me to date yet as an excuse to let him down gently. I'm not a guy, but I can imagine how devastating it is to ask a girl out only to be told by the girl she isn't interested in him "in that way." It's like telling him, "Sorry, but I think you're ugly and uninteresting."

After English, he asked me where his next class was, and I was actually kind of glad it wasn't the same one I was going to. That would have felt *really* weird, as if my fairy godmother was trying to tell me I needed to fall head-over-heels in love with him or something.

When I finally arrived home that afternoon and started on my homework after a snack, I found myself thinking of Nick. Not in a boyfriend kind of way but a friend kind of way. I was starting to realize he might be a really good friend to have.

It wasn't until months later I found out he had been thinking of me in the same way at the same time because as it turned out, he was really in need of a bestie as well. But for him it was about more than just having someone to talk to. It was urgent for him, even if neither of us realized how urgent at the time.

2

The next morning, I found myself looking forward to seeing Nick at school. It was the first time I had ever looked forward to seeing a boy more than another girl, and it felt weird, like there was something bad that might happen because of it. I knew I didn't like him as a boyfriend. For one thing, if he'd tried to kiss me I would have whacked him, and hard. There were boys I wouldn't whack if they'd tried to kiss me, so I knew it wasn't because I just didn't recognize the signs. And the weirdest part was that he wasn't bad looking at all. I just wasn't thinking of him like that.

Like I said, weird.

Anyway, as my mom was taking me to school, she noticed I was sort of thinking about other stuff, so she asked me about it, of course.

"What's up with you this morning? You've hardly said a word, and that's definitely not like you."

"Nothing," I said, hoping she would give it up and just drive.

"The surest bet in the world is that when someone says 'nothing' in response to that question, it's definitely something. It's just such a big something they don't want to talk about it."

I looked at her. "Okay, then it's something I don't want to talk about. At least not yet."

"A boy?"

My mom wouldn't let me date yet, but she knew that didn't keep me from thinking about boys.

"Yes and no."

"What's that mean?"

Later I realized my mom was an expert at getting me to talk about something I didn't want to talk about at all.

"It means I like him but not like that."

"Then why is he so much on your mind?"

"I don't know. That's sort of the problem. I know I don't *like* him, like him. But I can't seem to get him off my mind."

"Did I ever tell you about Ben?"

"Ben?"

"Yes. A boy I knew when I was a teenager."

"Was that around the time you ran off with that creep?"

"Yes."

I admired my mom for talking to me about that kind of thing. A lot of moms would never let their daughters know they had messed up that bad before, as if their daughters might think their moms were human or something. I sometimes got mad at my mom, but she was always straight with me. She said she told me about her mistakes so I wouldn't make the same ones. She also said she wanted me to know that everyone messes up all the time, but the important thing was learning from those mistakes and becoming a better person for having lived through the consequences. And her consequences had been real doozies.

"So who was this Ben?"

"He was a boy who was only a friend until I realized he could be more than that. I ended up dating him through high school."

"Was he good-looking?"

"Not particularly. I mean he wasn't ugly. He was just—I don't know—average, I guess you'd say, and a little on the chubby side."

"This was after the creep?"

"Yes. I learned that good looks weren't everything, for boys or girls. Who they are is more important than what they are."

I'd never really thought about that as it related to boys. Looks meant a lot to me back then as far as really liking a boy. I grew to understand what she meant, though, because of the girls. Some of the prettiest girls in school could be the ugliest as far as their personalities went, and I realized that went for boys, too.

"Did you love Ben?"

"I did, but it wasn't enough to marry him."

"What happened to him?"

"When we graduated from high school, he joined the Air Force. He ended up in Germany and met a girl that he married. We had broken up when he went in the Air Force anyway."

"So he didn't break your heart?"

"No, not in the least. I was happy for him."

"Do you hear from him now?"

"No."

"That's sad."

"It happens more than you realize. People drift apart, even people who care for each other."

I shrugged and looked out the window, still

thinking about Nick. Would I end up liking him in that way like my mom did with Ben? I sort of hoped not. I was needing a real friend, not someone who would get all caught up with the love thing. That would change everything. It always did.

My mom, though, wasn't finished. "So what about this guy? Does he have a name?"

"Of course he does. It's Nick."

"Does he have a last name?"

I was suddenly aware that I didn't know it. He was just Nick.

"Yes, he has a last name." I paused. "I just don't know it."

"So you're telling me you don't like this boy as a boyfriend but you've not spoken to him? Why not?"

"No. We've talked. I just don't know his last name. It never came up in the conversation."

"Does he know your last name?"

"Mom, could you drop it?" I didn't want to answer because I knew he didn't. I couldn't even remember if I told him my first name. Because I didn't like it, I sometimes avoided telling people at first.

"Okay. We're almost to the school anyway."

She pulled into the drop-off area, and I grabbed my bookbag and started to get out of the car.

"No kiss goodbye?" she asked.

Sighing, I leaned over to her and gave her a quick kiss on the cheek, which she returned. Before driving off, she smiled at me as if I'd just done a great trick or something.

Hefting my bookbag over my shoulder, I

walked into the building, aware that I was searching for Nick as I walked toward the cafeteria. The students were allowed to gather and talk there before the first bell.

I spotted Nick sitting alone at a table and walked up to him. It seemed strange that he wasn't trying to be friends with some of the guys in our class and stranger still that he wasn't trying to talk to any of the girls. Could he prefer being alone?

I decided to sit at his table since that seemed the friendly thing to do.

"Hey."

"Hi."

"What's up?"

He shrugged. "Hanging around 'til the first bell."

"By the way, I don't know your last name."

"I don't know yours either."

"Oh. Well, my last name is Lindstrom."

"Mine's Winslow."

I smiled at him and reached out a hand. "Nice to meet you Winslow."

He gave me a half-grin and said, "Nice to meet you, Lindstrom."

"Can I ask you a question?" I said. He looked at me, waiting, and I began to wonder if he'd be a good friend after all. He acted like words cost ten bucks apiece.

Finally, I asked, "Are you okay?" I realized after I said it that it might sound rude. "I mean, we've tried to be your friend and all, but you don't seem like you want any friends."

"We?"

"You know. Mia and Cameron and me."

"Oh, yeah."

"Especially Mia. She likes you, you know."

His face scrunched up like he was puzzled. "How could she like me like that when she barely knows me?"

"Because she thinks you're hot."

He frowned, as if that was ridiculous. Then he stared at the tabletop for a minute before answering. "No, I want friends. I just—" He allowed whatever he was going to say to disappear into his head. Then he must have realized he wasn't being very nice, so he said, "I guess I have some stuff to deal with and it's not that easy. I'm glad you want to be my friend."

"What kind of stuff?"

He grabbed his bookbag and started to stand up. "Family stuff. Look, I'm sorry. I do want to be your friend, but I don't really want to talk about this. It's kind of personal. I'll see you in science." With that, he turned and walked away, leaving me gaping at his back.

I wasn't sure what kind of family stuff would make someone act that way, but I figured it must be something really bad. He was acting like he wanted to curl up somewhere and die or something.

I looked around and saw Mia, who had apparently seen me talking to Nick. She was walking over to me like a locomotive, with the emphasis on the loco part.

"We need to talk!" she said.

"Look," I said, "I know you like Nick. I don't. At least not like that. If he starts coming on to me,

I'm going to let him know I don't like him in that way and maybe suggest he try to get to know you better. Okay?" I didn't mention how I'd told him she thought he was hot. That would have just made things worse.

Her stance softened a bit, but she was still glaring at me. "You don't like him?"

"Not like that. I just like him as a friend." She continued glaring, not sure I was telling the truth. "Honest!"

"If you're lying to me, you're going to regret it, Maureen." She slowly unfolded her arms and our little spat was forgotten for the moment. It would rear its ugly head several more times over the next few weeks, but we were friends again for now.

At the time, I thought Mia's reaction to me talking to Nick was a big problem for me. I know what big problems are now.

3

As Nick walked to his first class, he thought about what Maureen had said. On the one hand, he wanted friends, and Maureen seemed like a nice person. He was also flattered that Mia was interested in him.

The problem was he wasn't sure how long he would be in Denton. If they moved again, it would make the third move this year. He wasn't sure exactly why they kept moving like this. They'd lived in California for most of his life, but one day his father had come home and announced they were moving to Michigan, of all places. Nick had made friends there and was getting used to the new situation, but then his father had come home again one day and announced they were moving again. At least this time they were moving to Florida. Michigan was okay, but he hadn't been looking forward to the winter there.

Now, he was curious about why the sudden moves had happened in the first place. His brother Jimmy, who was ten, didn't seem all that bothered by the moves, but Nick wondered if he should even bother to make new friends. Would they be moving again in a few months? What if he fell in love with a girl like Mia? He'd never be able to speak to her again, and seeing her would definitely be out of the question.

Because that was one of his dad's rules. Once they left California, his father had demanded that they never contact their friends there again. All communications had been cut off with everyone he'd known. Now, he was forbidden from contacting his friends in Grand Rapids. He knew if they moved again, contact with anyone he met here would be banned as well.

The worst part was his dad had said nothing about why they were moving. Not from California. Not from Michigan. It was just, "We're moving." At least in Michigan, he'd had the decency to add "again" to the announcement.

He had asked his mom why they were moving when they left California, but she'd just said they had no choice. No explanation. Just that. When he'd asked why they had no choice, his mom had said he should just forget about it and, as she put it, "roll with it."

Nick was already tired of rolling.

As he sat in his first class, paying almost no attention to the teacher, he wondered if he should accept the friendship Maureen and the others had offered. He could see being part of their group would make him the envy of a lot of guys. The girls were all pretty. That envy would either cause guys to hate him or do their best to become a part of the group he hung around with—namely Maureen and the others.

But he also knew he was risking more than that. He'd only had time to call his lifelong best friend, Ray, when he'd learned they were moving to Michigan. All he was allowed to tell him was that they were moving, but not where. He'd been forced to tell him he didn't know where they were going. It was weird. His mom had even listened to his side of the conversation to make sure he didn't say anything about where they were going.

He considered now that maybe his dad was running from the law or something. Families didn't just leave the home they'd had for over a decade unless something drastic had happened. Were they in witness protection? Was someone trying to kill his father? He longed for answers to these questions but knew he couldn't ask them. If he did, he would just be told to "roll with it."

His next class was science, and he wanted to come to some decision about being friends with any of the girls at their science table before then. He didn't want to get a reputation as some dork who wasn't friendly, but he also didn't want to have to make friends and suddenly move without warning. It was a—he struggled for the word and then had it—a conundrum. As some adults would say, he was damned if he did and damned if he didn't.

That thought led him to realize if he was damned in either case, he should go ahead and make friends. He would just keep reminding himself not to get too close to anyone because leaving could be painful if he did.

When the bell rang to send him to science, he gathered his things and wondered if anything important had been covered in the history class he'd just sat through. He'd been too lost in thought to remember anything the teacher had said.

He stepped into the hall and saw Mia nearby,

sort of standing there, looking as if she had something she needed to do but couldn't remember what it was. He wondered if she were just waiting for him to come out of class to walk with him to science. Part of him was happy about this, but another part was worried. *You can't fall for her*, he reminded himself. *You can like her but you can't fall for her.*

"Hi!" she said, as if surprised to see him. "I didn't know you had Lovelace for history first class! I have him for sixth period."

"History?"

"Yeah."

"Good, maybe later you can share what went on in class today. I was too busy thinking about things to pay attention."

"What kind of things?"

"Nothing big," he lied. "Want to walk together to science?" He hoped the offer would leave the subject of what he'd been thinking about behind forever.

"Sure! I mean, we're both going there, so of course."

As they walked he could feel her looking at him. He turned his head toward her, catching her before she looked away, blushing a bit.

Apparently, Maureen had been telling the truth. Mia did seem to like him.

As he sat with Mia at their table, he could tell Maureen and Cameron noticed they had walked in together.

"Wow, that was fast!" Cameron said.

"Shut up, Cameron!" Mia said, an obvious

warning.

Class began, and Nick did his best to fit in rather than stick to himself. It was a good feeling, but at the same time, he wondered how long these friendships would last.

4

When I woke up that Saturday, my mom told me she needed to talk to me about something. I wasn't thrilled about this since when people say that, it's never good. I was right. I listened to what she had to say as a sense of dread flooded over me.

"Maureen, I know you won't like this, but your grandmother is coming to live with us."

She was right. I love my grandmother. I just don't like her very much.

"Why does she have to live with us?"

"For a number of reasons. She has some health issues and while she can live by herself, it's best if she lives with someone."

"Can't we get someone to move in with her?"

"No. She's moving in with us. Get used to it."

"When?"

"Wednesday."

Great. I had four more days of no tension in the house until she arrived.

My grandmother was one of those people who maybe should have skipped having kids, but then if she had, I wouldn't be here. Still, my mom told me stories of when she was growing up when her mother wasn't exactly nice to her and often took the side of her second husband over my mom.

I had always avoided her if I could. I remember

one time when I was little, I made her a picture of flowers in a garden. Okay, I was little, maybe five, so I'm sure it wasn't a Monet, but instead of telling me how much she liked it, she found fault with it. She went on about things like perspective, which I didn't understand at all. I mean, it was a little kid's drawing of a field of flowers.

I had colored the sky blue, but only up at the top of the picture because to a kid my age, the sky was "up." I remember she took me outside and pointed up at the sky. She said, "You see the blue up there?"

"Yes."

Then she pointed at the horizon. "Do you see the blue where the sky reaches the earth?"

"Yes."

She handed me back my drawing. "Then your sky should do the same."

I was devastated. I mean, she'd never been the nicest person in the world to me or anything, but finding problems with what I had done just to please her crushed me.

I never made her another picture, and I never forgot how wounded to the core her comments made me feel.

People sometimes think a little kid that age won't remember stuff like that, but we do. Or they think we'll get over it in a few minutes. We don't. Crushed feelings scar the soul and make the heart stop beating for a second. Apologizing is just an ointment that makes it feel better for a moment, but the permanent damage has been done.

After learning my grandmother would be living

with us, I spent that day moping, and to my mother's credit, she allowed me to as long as I didn't bother her anymore with the topic. To her, it was a closed discussion, and she was right. I mean, who listens to a thirteen-year-old about things like that?

The only thing that happened to interrupt my misery was something that was only a little bit less miserable. Cameron called with the latest Nick and Mia news: apparently, they were going to a movie together that afternoon. I really didn't care and was happy for both of them, but Cameron was acting like the news was that people had landed on Mars or something.

I stayed on the call mostly because it kept me from thinking about my grandmother. Finally, though, Mom saw me on the phone for the second time during that same call and looked at her watch.

"I think it's time to give the phone a rest," she said.

I said goodbye to Cameron and then found my mom in what had been the guest room but would now be my grandmother's. She was getting the room ready for her.

"You know, if you'd get me my own cell phone, I wouldn't have to tie up the house phone," I said, hoping maybe this time she would relent, but no dice. "Most people don't even have a house phone these days."

"You don't need a cell phone. You just need to find other things to do with your time," she said, giving me that "not on your life" look she seems to have patented. "Why not read a book?"

That was kind of funny, really. My mom was diagnosed as ADHD when she was a kid and has told me how much trouble she had reading a book when she was young. Now, though, she reads a lot partly because she takes her meds every day. She says it only goes to show how much people can change as they grow up, but I know better. She had help becoming a reader.

When she was in her mid-teens, Mr. Turner, the lawyer who helped her, made a deal with her. If she would read a whole book—not a kid's book but a high school or older book that he would choose—he would give her twenty dollars, but she had to pass a test on the book to collect.

She took him up on it and read the book he gave her, *The Outsiders* by S. E. Hinton. It wasn't a long book and my mom read it in only a few days, telling Mr. Turner that it was the first time she'd read a book she liked so much she couldn't put it down. She told me this story to try to urge me to read it, but so far I haven't seen her pony up any money for me to do it, so I'm holding out.

Wednesday evening arrived along with my grandmother, who before that day had lived in an apartment across town. She seemed about as happy to be living with us as I was to have her there. This made me mad since we were making a big adjustment to our lives for her and she didn't seem to care.

My mom had told me that when she drove up the driveway with Grandma, I should come out and welcome her and help bring in her belongings. I'm sure it didn't go as my mother had planned.

"Hey, Grandma!" I said, doing my best to be cheerful. "Come to stay with us awhile?" It was the only thing I could think to say.

"For the rest of my life, apparently."

I hefted her suitcase from the opened trunk and tried to ignore her.

"Be careful with that! I have some breakable keepsakes in there."

As I went up the front steps, the suitcase banged against the top step.

"I said be careful!"

"I'm doing the best I can! You don't like how I'm doing it, you can carry it in yourself. It weighs a ton!"

"Maureen!" Mom said, warning me.

"Well, she always complains about anything I do, even when I'm trying to help!"

"Your attitude isn't helping a bit," Mom said.

"Neither is hers!"

Grandma brushed past me and went inside, leaving Mom and me to sort it out, I guess.

Mom walked up to me so she could talk without being heard inside. "I've told you we need to make the best of this situation. She's here and that's that. I'll not have arguments every single day."

"Fine," I said and lifted the suitcase as high as I could to make sure it didn't bump against anything. Grandma was in her sixties, but there was not much wrong with her hearing, and I could imagine what she might say if she heard the suitcase bump against something again.

I lugged the bag into the room where Grandma would be living, as she put it, for the rest of her life and went upstairs to my room. Plopping on my bed, I took out my journal. I sat thinking about what I should write but decided I was too angry to write anything. It wasn't that I worried someone might find it and read it. Mom knew I kept a journal and promised she wouldn't read it if she ever found it, and Grandma would have to get a stepladder to get to it on the top shelf of my closet, where I'd moved it that morning from my bedside drawer. No, I just knew I would rather not read what I might write once I'd calmed down.

It's like one time I wrote this horrible thing about Mia and regretted it the next day. I ended up tearing out the pages and having to write the first part of what I tore out again because it had nothing to do with Mia and I wanted to keep that part.

Besides, my mom had told me that it was best to give myself time when I was angry about something to get perspective. I was used to her telling me things like that. She called them "Dawsonisms" after the woman she'd worked for when she was a teenager, Mrs. Mary Jane Dawson.

Mom had told me if I wanted to write something worth keeping in my journal, I should write down the Dawsonisms she told me. After thinking about it, I realized maybe she was right, so I started writing down all of them I could.

Mrs. Dawson had died when I was two, and though I'd met her, I didn't remember her. Mom said that was too bad because she was a great lady. She was in her nineties when she died, so at least she had a long life. All I know is that my mom adored her, along with a lawyer who still lives here named Jack Turner. I'd met Mr. Turner and his wife. They were nice and referred to my mom as their adopted daughter. There were times I wished that was true, like now.

Since I was so angry, I decided to read a few Dawsonisms to see if that might improve my mood. That was weird, too, because the very first one I saw was about anger.

You see, whenever I felt like reading some Dawsonisms, I would turn to one of the pages at the back of my journal where I kept them, close my eyes, and place my finger somewhere on the page. I would open my eyes and read the one I was pointing at.

This time, it was like God Himself was speaking to me. "Anger, especially anger at something nobody can do anything about, doesn't hurt anyone but the angry person."

I think my jaw might have dropped open. Then I looked at the next one and blushed. "Sex is wonderful, but it can be a nightmare if shared with the wrong person." I was only thirteen. I didn't need this one yet at all.

But that first one—boy did I need to hear that.

My anger at my grandmother disappeared almost immediately. Of course, it would return soon. Not returning when it came to my grandmother was nearly impossible. But it was gone for now.

I considered what I might write before turning back to the end of the last entry and beginning to write.

Why does my grandmother not like me? It's like she goes out of her way to be angry with me over nothing. She moved in with us today because, as my mom put it, she had to. I don't know the full story on that. 'She had to' could mean a lot. Mom mentioned it was for several reasons, including her health. What other reasons? Was she unable to afford to live alone anymore? Was she somehow in danger like some people wanted to kill her and she needed to move out of her apartment? Who knows? Anyway, I'm not happy about it, and Grandma isn't either, and I can't help but think her being unhappy about it has something to do with me, like she would be okay living with my mom, but living with me is a problem. I would ask her about it, but that would just lead to an argument. Or should I say another argument? We seem to have them every time we talk. I honestly think I could ask her what she thinks of the weather and we'd end up in an argument. It's kind of sad when you think about it. My mom asked me to try to be nice, but I think that's a two-way street.

Shouldn't Grandma try to be nice, too? I mean, if I have to, I think she should, too. It's only fair.

I remembered another Dawsonism and considered crossing out that last sentence. It was a Dawsonism I'd heard from a lot of other people, too. "Life isn't fair. Get used to it."

That didn't stop me from wanting it to be fair, so I kept it.

I reread what I'd written and was satisfied with it. Just as I had finished putting my journal back on the shelf in my closet, I heard the phone ring. Mom answered it and called upstairs to my bedroom.

"Maureen! Phone!"

I opened my door. "I'll take it up here!" I went to my mom's bedroom to use the phone by her bed while wishing again she'd buy me a cell phone.

"Hello?"

Silence, then, "Hey."

It was Nick. I hoped this was a call because he thought of me as a friend and not a girlfriend. That could get awkward. Oddly, the Dawsonism about sex went through my mind even though sex with Nick was about the last thing I would ever do. I blushed just from thinking about it and was glad he couldn't see me.

"Hey, Nick. What's up?" I asked, hoping this would be just some meaningless chitchat between new friends.

"I think I need to talk to someone and thought you might be willing to listen."

Okay. Maybe this wouldn't be some meaningless chitchat. He sounded really serious, like he had some awful confession and was counting on me to be okay with whatever it was.

It made me take a few deep breaths. Then I calmed myself, thinking this was probably something about Mia and their budding relationship. I could handle that.

"Sure," I said. "What's going on?"

I heard a deep sigh and then he said, "Listen, what I'm about to tell you has to stay just between us, okay? I asked around at school, and people said you're not a gossip. Is that true?"

"If you mean do I blab everything someone tells me, no. I know how to keep a secret."

"You're not just saying that so I'll tell you?"

"No."

"Okay. Here goes." Another sigh. "Things aren't real great for me."

"Oh?" I wondered if Mia had broken up with him already.

"Yeah. You see, we've moved suddenly twice in the past several months. First from California to Michigan. Then from Michigan to here."

"Why?"

"That's just it. I don't know. My parents won't share why with me or my brother."

"You have a brother?"

"Yeah. He's ten. It doesn't seem to bother him, but it's got me spooked. Like what if we move again in a couple of months? All the friends I made here would just sort of disappear."

"I won't," I said and meant it. My heart went

out to Nick and I wanted to make him feel better. Besides, he was trusting me with a secret, though I had no idea why it should be so private. Still, he was trusting me, and that meant a lot.

"But when we move, I'm sort of forbidden from contacting anyone from where we lived before."

"That's weird."

"Tell me about it. So, you see, even if we become the best friends ever, I wouldn't be able to contact you again if we move. You'd lose all contact with me."

"What about email?"

"I'm not allowed to have it."

No email? What kind of family did Nick come from? It made my problems with my grandmother seem small.

"Do you have a cell phone?"

"No."

Join the club, I thought. At least this made it where I wasn't the only kid my age I knew who didn't have one.

"Why do you think y'all have to move so much?"

"I don't know, but it's always a big rush. I mean, my dad will come home and say, "We're moving." The next day, we move. We rent furnished houses because we had to leave our furniture in California."

I thought about that a moment when an idea hit me so hard it made me gasp.

"What?" he asked.

"Is it possible your dad's in witness protection

or something, and people find out who he really is?"

"I don't think so. Wouldn't that mean he had gone to court as a witness? I don't think he's done that."

"How would you know? It's not like he'd get everyone together for a picnic and testimony at the courthouse or something."

"I don't know. I mean my dad has a boring job. It just doesn't seem like he'd be a witness to much of anything."

"What does he do?"

"He's an accountant."

He was right. That sounded boring to me, too. Numbers were never very interesting to me, though I guess the world needs accountants, so it's good it doesn't sound boring to everyone.

"Is he acting like he's going to move again?"

"That's just it. There's never any warning."

"It's only happened twice, though. Maybe you just weren't picking up the signals."

"No, there were no signals. He just came home and announced we were moving."

"How long did you live in California?"

"I was born there. My parents owned a house there and everything. Then one day—POOF!—we were moving to Michigan. Then about three months later—POOF again—we're moving to Florida."

"That is weird. I'm so sorry."

"Yeah. I just wanted to let you know why I'm so worried about making new friends and all. And now, well, I kind of like Mia. She even let me kiss her last weekend when we went to a movie. In fact, we barely watched the movie. We just sat in the back row and made out." Another pause, then he said, "I hope that doesn't, like, make you jealous or anything. You said you just wanted to be my friend, right?"

"No jealousy here," I said and meant it. In the back of my mind, I wondered if I should share the Dawsonism about sex with either Nick or Mia—or both. It sounded like if they didn't slow it down a bit, they'd be parents sometime in the next year, and that wouldn't be good for anyone.

I decided not to share the Dawsonism but I did say, "Nick, you might need to be careful. Mia can be a little on the wild side, and you're both too young to become parents."

"Parents? No way! I mean that. I never want kids."

I let it drop by saying. "I didn't mean it's definitely going to happen. I was just warning you. You know, like a friend should."

He was silent for a moment before saying, "Okay. I guess I should thank you for thinking about my future or something."

"Listen, if somehow you end up somewhere else, you can email me from a library computer."

"But I told you that I'm not allowed to have an email address."

"So? Who has to know? Just me and you. Look, I'll set one up for you on Gmail. You can change the password after I set it up. That way, we can still stay in touch no matter what happens."

"I don't know," he said.

"But I do. Look, it's just email. It's almost impossible to find out who the person really is."

"Okay. I guess that will work."

"Of course it will. Just leave it all up to your BFF." I smiled when I said that.

I was only thirteen and had no idea what I was starting, though.

5

I survived the first night with my grandmother living there. We had dinner together "as a family" my mother said. For the life of me, I couldn't understand why Grandma was there if she didn't want to be, which was obvious. And even more than that, I wondered why my mom, who seemed equally uncomfortable with this new arrangement, wanted Grandma there.

Even at dinner, Grandma didn't speak unless she needed something.

"Could someone pass the salt," she said to nobody in particular, as if my mom and I were in a contest to see who could please her.

"Mom, your blood pressure," my mother warned.

"Will start rising if you refuse me salt," Grandma answered.

Mom sighed and passed the salt shaker. Grandma took it and sprinkled salt on her food as though it was her last chance to use any for the rest of her life. I grimaced at the amount she was using, wondering how she would taste the food with that much salt on it.

After dinner, Grandma retired to her room while Mom and I watched some TV. We were watching an episode of Law and Order SVU when Grandma passed the TV room on her way to the kitchen for something to drink. "You let her watch this garbage?" Grandma said.

"It's not garbage. It's a good show," Mom said.

"It's about sex," Grandma said.

"Not really. It's about sex crimes and how easy it is to be lured into being a victim."

"Still, she's only thirteen," Grandma said, as if I wasn't there or I couldn't understand English or something.

Mom looked at Grandma. "Maybe if you'd let me watch shows like this when I was thirteen, things might have been different."

That shut Grandma up. I was sure my mom was referring to the guy she ran off with to Jacksonville. She'd even told me that she felt closer to Jack and Jenny Turner and Mrs. Dawson after she finally made it back home after her trial than she did to her mom. I could understand.

When the show was over, I asked Mom to turn off the TV because I felt we needed to talk about stuff. She shut it off as if expecting me to ask.

She turned to me in silence. "Mom? What's going on? She doesn't want to be here, and it's kind of obvious you don't really want her here, either."

She gave me a sad look and took a deep breath before resettling herself on the sofa to be able to face me better.

"There are a number of reasons, really. She has some health issues that would make it better if she didn't live alone. But it's more than just that. Baby, this is my last chance, and maybe yours, too."

"Last chance for what?"

"To—well—make amends with my mother."

"She doesn't seem anxious to do that, either."

"Maybe not, but I'm hoping she'll change her mind. You see, we've been at odds for a long time now. Believe it or not, my relationship with my mother improved for a while after I came home from Jacksonville, but then things...changed."

"How? What happened?"

Mom took another deep breath. I could tell she didn't really want to talk about this but felt she needed to. My heart went out to her when I thought of that. I realized she may have some doubts about how much her mother loved her, but I had no such problem knowing how much my mom loved me. She was talking to me about this because she knew I needed to hear it. It didn't make her comfortable to talk about it, but she loved me enough to do it anyway.

It was like the sex talk we'd had when I was eleven and my body had started changing. Mom had talked to me about a lot of stuff then, even some really personal stuff that made me blush, but at the same time, I had admired her for being willing to talk to me about things like that despite it making both of us uncomfortable. She'd said she wanted me to be informed about what was happening to my body as well as my mind and not to be ashamed or embarrassed about any of it. I loved her for that.

"Honey, when I got back from Jacksonville, I was thrilled to be home. My mom and brother were thrilled, too. The man who became my stepfather could be difficult, though. In fact, he could go from being nice to becoming hostile towards me, often reminding me how much heartache I'd caused and

39

how bad a person I was."

"Why would Grandma marry him if he was like that?"

"She was lonely. My father had disappeared, running off with a younger woman. Her ego had been shattered. I didn't realize it then. I was too immature and self-centered. My mom had never allowed me to learn anything about how destructive life can be, so I had become an easy target myself. The boy I'd left behind in North Carolina would have used me until he was finished and tossed me aside, but I didn't realize that. I ended up with an even worse boyfriend—one who became like a slave master."

She paused a moment. "My mom and I were a lot alike, as it turned out. So when she was faced with backing me up or making a sometimes hateful man she loved happy, she chose the latter."

"I'm sorry."

"Well, the way I look at it, it all made me who I am today. And one thing I am is someone willing to let bygones be bygones and see if I can salvage some kind of relationship with my mother." She sighed deeply. "And I want you to have that chance, too. Down deep, she's a good person. She's just bitter sometimes how her life worked out."

"Do you think she loves me?" I asked.

To her credit, she didn't answer right away. If she had, I might not have believed her.

She nodded. "Yes, I think she does, but she's been hurt a lot in life, much of that pain being caused by me, and she's—I don't know—wary, I guess, would be the word."

"How did you hurt her? I mean, once you came back from Jacksonville."

"I moved out of the house."

This was news. I had never known she'd done that. "Where did you live? On the streets?" I could suddenly picture my mom living under some overpass somewhere in Wharton, the larger town a few miles west of Denton.

She smiled. "No. I moved in with Mrs. Dawson."

I suddenly felt like I was meeting my mom for the first time or something. She had never mentioned this to me.

"On the one hand, it improved me and my life, but on the other, it was the wrong thing to do."

"How so?"

"Because, baby, I was just avoiding my problems with my mother."

"You've thought about this a lot, haven't you?"

She nodded. "That's why I insisted my mother move in with us. She wasn't in favor of it, but I begged her to. She agreed to give it a try."

"So she knows that's what this is about? That you want us all to make amends?"

"Yes, and the fact she has issues related to getting old."

I looked at the doorway to the hall where Grandma had been standing a short time ago, complaining about the show Mom was letting me watch.

"She doesn't seem to be trying very hard."

She shrugged. "We have to give it time. This isn't easy for any of us."

She could say that again. "I love you, Mom."

She held out her arms. I was on the opposite end of the sofa, so I scooted over next to her. She hugged me and gave me a kiss on top of my head as she urged me to lie against her with my back to her right side. "I love you, too, baby."

We sat like that for a while before I got up and said, "I guess I need to get to bed."

"Yep. School night."

I left the room and as I walked toward the stairs to go up to my room, I noticed light coming from beneath the door to Grandma's room. She was still up. I hesitated, debating if I should do what I was considering. Then, deciding I had to start somewhere, I went to her door and tapped lightly, hoping she would answer as well as hoping she wouldn't.

"Yes?" she said.

I cracked the door open a few inches. She was lying in bed, reading. "Goodnight, Grandma," I said.

Without changing her expression, she said, "Goodnight."

It wasn't much, but it had been a civil exchange, at least. She didn't sound happy that I'd stopped to say goodnight, but she didn't seem irritated or upset either. It was just—polite. I counted it as a step in the right direction.

Closing her door, I made my way up to my room and changed into my pajamas. As I lay in bed that night, I thought of what my mom had told me, especially how she had moved out of her house to live with Mrs. Dawson. I wondered how much leaving her mother and brother had hurt my mom.

As I fell asleep, I thought of Nick and his situation. It felt weird that his family would make sudden decisions to move without any warning. I again wondered if his father might be in the witness protection program. That would explain it, I suppose, and it seemed easy for the government to find a job for an accountant in a different town.

The next morning when I arrived at school, I went to find Nick. He was in the cafeteria, sitting with Mia. Cameron hadn't arrived yet.

Just glancing at them, I could see she was a lot more into him than he was into her. I wondered how much the constant threat to move was responsible for his holding back. Probably a lot. After all, hadn't he said they had more or less missed the movie because they'd been making out in the back row of the theater? Now, though, he looked like he wasn't sure he wanted to know her.

What was also funny was that he didn't recognize the jealousy of the guys at school. Mia was one of those girls the guys were always frothing at the mouth over. Even I knew that Mia wasn't a prude and would have no problem with a guy touching her in some intimate places if she liked him, and the boys in the school knew that, too. She had a bit of a reputation. She wouldn't go "all the way" with someone, but heavy petting was not out of the question.

That's another way she and I are different. If some guy had even looked like he was about to get too intimate, I'd have belted him. The kids knew that, too. Once a boy named Kyle had tried to kiss me at a pep rally, and I slapped him. It left a red handprint on his cheek, and I'd said, "I only get kissed if I want to get kissed!" It had sent a clear message to the guys I knew. *Don't mess with Maureen Lindstrom* had become a well-known saying among the boys at school.

I didn't want to talk to Nick with Mia there about the email address I'd created for him after our phone call the night before. She would have been suspicious that I was trying to set up some kind of personal interactions between him and me, so I had to wait until English class.

When we were safely in Ms. Henderson's room, I leaned across to him and said, "Here, take this."

The small piece of paper I handed him had a Gmail address and the password for it. Below that, I'd written, "Change the password after you open the Gmail account. I've sent you an email. Reply when you open it." Below that, I'd written, "Memorize the address and password then destroy this!"

I'd made the account and password easy to memorize. The password was NickWinslow1. The Gmail account was NickisNice and the zip code for Denton. He tore the paper into small bits and threw them in the wastebasket in Ms. Henderson's room.

The email I'd sent him was mostly about how I liked him as a friend and how sad it was he was scared about suddenly moving away. I included some ideas about why his family might have moved so much, focusing on witness protection. By the time I got home and had a snack, an email was waiting for me in my inbox. I smiled as I opened it.

Maureen,

Thanks for this. I guess I could have set it up on my own, but I sort of don't think I would have. Somehow, it feels wrong to do this behind my parents back but what could it hurt, right? At least now I can communicate with friends. I have email addresses for friends in California, so I should be able to get in touch with them now, too, if I decide to. I'll have to think about it. Thanks again.

Your MBFF (male best friend forever),
Nick

I grinned at the closing and cringed inwardly at the missing apostrophe after "parents." But I had a BFF, even if it was a guy. I thought it was funny how he'd added the "M" with an explanation so I wouldn't wonder about it.

I sat thinking for a while about how weird it was that he hadn't created an email address before. He knew the email addresses of friends in places he'd lived before—friends he missed a lot, according to him—and I felt that creating an email account would have been the first thing I did when I'd reached Grand Rapids.

I thought about this and realized that mostly I was right with my choice of a Gmail account name. Nick was nice. So nice he hadn't gone behind his parents' backs to create an email account because they'd not allowed him to do that.

And what was with that? Why would they not allow him to contact his friends? If his dad was in witness protection, it wasn't like anyone would know where Nick was from an email, right? Okay, maybe there was some way to find out that I didn't know, but who would be monitoring that, anyway? Would someone be watching all the email providers' sites for someone named Nick to open an account? How could they be sure it was that particular Nick?

After homework and dinner, Mom insisted we all three play a game of rummy together. Grandma was pleasant, even if she wasn't overly friendly or even moderately happy to be playing any kind of game with us, but she did it anyway. That she seemed to be at least trying made me happy.

That night, I lay in bed thinking of the email thing again. I only wish I'd known how terribly wrong I was about how easy it would be to trace an email. It would have saved me a lot of heartache and Nick's family a lot of problems, too.

6

Nick sat in the public library in Denton that Saturday and stared at the blank email screen. He wanted to email Ray, his best friend from California, but still wasn't sure he should. That his parents had forbidden him to email or contact anyone after leaving the home they'd had since Nick was born preyed on his mind. They must have had a reason for doing that, didn't they? Would he mess something up by emailing Ray? He couldn't imagine how that could be possible, but still he wondered.

The weirdest part of all was that when they left California, he'd only known they were moving to Michigan with no mention of the city. Were his parents really on the run? What if they were running from the law? Had his mom or dad committed a felony? That didn't seem possible, but he knew it could be possible after all.

But why couldn't he tell Ray? It wasn't like Ray was going to blab it to anyone. Besides, how would anyone know to even ask Ray if he knew where they were? If his parents had done something or were on the run for some reason, the police or whoever would be asking adults who knew his parents, not kids.

Finally, he leaned toward the computer and began to type:

Hello, Ray-Man!

Bet you never expected to hear from me again, did you? To be honest, I sorta wondered myself. My life's been kinda weird since we left Benicia. Now, I'm gonna tell you where we've been since then, but you can't tell anyone. Not even your parents. I know you'll keep this quiet. You've proved you can keep a secret since we were little, so you just have to keep this one, too. Cool? Okay. When we left Benicia, we moved all the way to Grand Rapids, Michigan. To say I was bummed would be like saying I got a little damp in a rainstorm. It gets COLD in Michigan! Not to worry, though. We've moved again since then. Yep. We stayed in GR for all of a couple months. That's the coolest part. We're in Florida now! Freaking Florida! We moved to this town on the Gulf Coast called Denton. I've met these girls, and I think you'd really like one of them. Her name is Maureen. Yeah, I know. The name is kinda old fashioned, but she's really cool. She has a friend named Mia who's my girlfriend. She's hotter than a day at the beach! We went to a movie last weekend and I can't even tell you the name b/c we sat in the back row and made out during the entire movie! Anyway, that's where I am now. Just don't tell ANYONE where I am! My folks must have a reason for not wanting me to tell, but I know I can trust you!

L8r, Dude!

Nick

Nick re-read the email and hesitated, his finger on the mouse to press the "send" button. Then, deciding it couldn't possibly cause a problem, he clicked, and the email disappeared into the e-world.

Over two-thousand miles away outside San Francisco, a computer beeped. A technician named Landers clicked a few buttons and an email popped up. His bosses had hacked a number of email accounts for various reasons, some financial, some for security reasons. This email account had been hacked for what his boss had called a "level 4 security situation," involving Brad Winslow, an accountant who'd moved away suddenly after a breach in their security had occurred. Landers had no knowledge of what Winslow knew, but a level 4 meant it was top priority to find him and secure the breach. That meant the higher-ups were especially interested in emails arriving in one of the accounts that held certain types of information.

At first, he nearly ignored the email. It was to a kid. The tech wasn't sure why they would be monitoring a kid's email. Then again, a kid was more likely to mess up and email a friend, revealing something they wanted to know. He'd specifically been told to look for locations mentioned in any emails to this particular account. When he saw the mention of Grand Rapids and a town in Florida, he reached for the desktop phone and punched in a few numbers. When it was answered, he said, "Paige? Landers here. Is Adams available?"

"Sure. Hang on," Paige answered, and he was placed on hold for a few seconds.

"Yeah?" Ben Adams, his boss, answered.

"I think we might have something you want to see. One of the emails we're monitoring on the

Winslow situation just got one. It appears to be from one of Winslow's kids. I figured you'd want to know because it mentions a location."

"What location?"

"Apparently, they're in a town called Denton in Florida."

"Denton?"

"Yeah. I checked and it's on the northern Gulf Coast in the Panhandle."

Landers could almost hear the smile in his boss's response. "Thanks, Landers. Let me know if anything else develops."

Ben Adams hung up before immediately dialing another number. When his boss, David Bender, picked up, he said, "Mr. Bender? Adams here. I think we have where Winslow is holed up." After explaining what Landers had just shared, he waited for further instructions.

After a few seconds, Bender said, "Notify Osbourne. Tell him where to find Winslow. He'll know what to do."

After hanging up, David Bender sat for a moment thinking about Brad Winslow, a man who had worked for the firm as an accountant until he had discovered some details that could cost the firm dearly, not to mention himself. These details could ruin the company and cost the partners millions of dollars and probably send all of them, including Bender, to prison for at least a decade.

Winslow had been stupid enough to report his findings to his boss, who notified Bender. The fact Winslow disappeared with his entire family the day after discussing these illegal activities had left them with only one alternative that involved a man Bender knew only as "Osbourne," a man Bender had used once before to dispose of a problem. They'd managed to trace Winslow and his family to Grand Rapids when Winslow had phoned his brother, but they had left there suddenly as well, and the trail had gone cold.

Now, they had new information about his whereabouts, and Osbourne would be paying Winslow a visit that would prevent Winslow from telling anyone about his discovery. Since the authorities would have been in contact within days of finding out what Winslow had discovered, Bender knew that Winslow hadn't told anyone— yet. All Bender knew was that sending Osbourne was his only option.

7

When Saturday came, I sat in my room looking out the window at the rain. Mom had to work today. She and her assistant manager of the nursery Mom owned alternated Saturdays off, and this was Mom's weekend to work. They were closed Sundays, thankfully, so I would only have to spend this one day alone with my grandmother.

I went to my computer and logged in and checked the weather forecast. The rain was supposed to end by one that afternoon, so the day wouldn't be a total washout.

Deciding to call Cameron to see if she wanted to get together that afternoon, I walked down the short hallway to Mom's bedroom to use the upstairs phone for privacy. It wasn't that I would be saying anything all that private. It was just that I didn't want Grandma in my business.

However, as I stepped into Mom's room, I found Grandma was already there. She was snooping through Mom's stuff as if she had some sort of right to do that.

"Excuse me!" I said. "What are you doing?"

Grandma's head jerked around, guilt shaping and coloring her features.

"Oh. I was—I was looking for something."

"Like what?"

"Nothing really. It's not important. You needn't

concern yourself."

"I'm not concerned about what you were looking for as much as I am that you were snooping through Mom's things. This is her room!" I pointed at the open drawer Grandma had been pawing through. "That's her drawer." Storming over to where Grandma was standing, I reached inside the drawer, grabbing some of Mom's underwear in a clenched fist. Holding them up, I nearly shouted, "This is *her* stuff!" Tossing it back in, I said, "Why would you be searching for underwear anyway?"

"I wasn't searching for underwear, Maureen."

"Then what? Because it sure looks like you were searching through her underwear drawer to me!"

"Nothing!" she said and shoved past me.

"I'm going to tell her what you were doing!"

She turned to me. "She's no saint, you know. She's done more than run off with Travis Daly to Jacksonville."

I was surprised she said that. Now, I knew the name of the guy she ran off with. My mom had said he didn't deserve a name. Apparently, Grandma thought different.

"I know she's no saint, but she's a better mom than you because she managed to leave and live with Mrs. Dawson."

She stepped closer and slapped me. Hard. The stinging on my cheek moved to my eyes. I wanted to hit her back but knew I couldn't.

Perhaps she was afraid I might hit her, or maybe she was just tired of dealing with me. In any case, she turned and marched out the bedroom door. I heard her moving down the stairs, each step a thump that echoed like the beating of a war drum. I was furious, madder than I'd been in a long time. I wanted to call Mom at work but knew I couldn't unless, as she had always put it, I was bleeding and needed to go to the hospital. This wasn't an emergency. It was just me wanting my mom.

I sat on my mom's bed and cried. How could I ever love a woman who was like this? She obviously hated me, and I hated her so much right then that I made a silent wish that she would drop dead of a heart attack.

I knew I didn't mean it, though. That would hurt my mom too much. Still, I knew I didn't want to speak to her again that day.

I looked around the room and again wondered what Grandma had been looking for. The drawer still stood open, a pair of my mom's panties draped over the edge and sticking out like it wanted to escape the drawer.

That thought actually made me laugh, in spite of my anger. The laugh didn't last long, but it made me feel better. That was another Dawsonism: a little bit of laughter is an excellent cure for feeling down.

I began to wish for the thousandth time that Mrs. Dawson was alive and had been my grandmother instead of the witch living in our house. The way Mom described Mrs. Dawson, she *was* a saint. According to Mom, she loved baseball, beer, Mr. and Ms. Turner, and Mom. Oh, and her dog. Mom says she always loved dogs and would talk about each one she'd had since she was a little girl. When she died, Mr. Turner and his wife took in the dog she'd left behind. They loved dogs, too.

I wanted a dog really bad. It would be a companion who would love me no matter what was happening. Mom had had one before, but she says when the dog died, she was so upset she didn't want another one. So even though I wanted one, I knew I'd never have one. At least not until I was old enough to move out on my own.

Remembering why I'd come into Mom's bedroom in the first place, I reached for the phone to call Cameron. The call went to her voicemail without even ringing, so I knew she either had her phone turned off or she was talking to someone else. I left a message to call me back.

About a half hour later, the phone rang. I sprinted from my room to Mom's room and picked up.

"Hello?"

"Hey! Whatcha need?" Cameron said.

"I wondered if you wanted to get together this afternoon and do something."

"Like what?"

"Anything, as long as we do it somewhere besides here."

We chatted and made plans to meet in town at the Dairy Queen, deciding we could make up our minds what to do while we shared a sundae.

We chatted some more and then the call-waiting thing beeped on our phone.

"I gotta go," I said. "Someone's trying to call."

"Okay. See you at DQ later!"

I answered the other call. It was from Nick.

"Hey," he said after I answered. "What's up?"

"Not much." I didn't want to mention DQ

because I didn't want him to join Cameron and me. It would make Mia jealous.

He told me about how he emailed his friend in California and that he'd received a reply. Then he thanked me for helping him out.

"No problem," I said.

"How's it going with your grandmother?"

Okay. Touchy subject, even on the best day. But he was my MBFF. I just didn't know if he'd understand. I had considered talking to Cameron about it. She was a girl and might be more sympathetic. I wasn't sure. After realizing that was sexist, I gave it a try.

"Not so good."

"Oh?"

"Yeah. We had a fight."

"You guys argue much?"

"It was more than an argument. She slapped me."

"Wow. Why?"

I told him about finding her searching through my mom's stuff and what happened, leaving out a few details that I felt weren't important, like how I said my mom had done better for herself by moving in with Mrs. Dawson.

"Oh, man. I'm sorry," he said when I'd finished. "What do you think she was looking for?"

"I'm not sure, but I'm glad I hide my journal."

"You keep a journal, too?"

That one surprised me.

"Yeah. I never met a guy who kept one, though."

"Yeah. It was suggested by—well, it was suggested I try it."

I wasn't sure who suggested it, but he obviously didn't want to say, so I ignored that part.

"Does it help any?"

"Help with what?" His voice changed when he said that, like he didn't like my question.

"You know. Did it help you feel any better about things? That's why I keep one. Getting my feelings out on paper makes me feel better about stuff. Like my grandma living with us."

"Oh. Yeah, I guess it does. I haven't killed myself yet." He laughed a little, but his comment sounded a little serious, too, like maybe he'd thought of doing that and the laugh was sort of an attempt to hide that.

Instead of calling him on it or asking about it, I said, "Well, obviously" and laughed myself.

We chatted for a little more and he said he had to call Mia. When I asked why he called me before calling Mia, he said, "She told me to call at noon exactly."

"She's seeing if she has you wrapped around her little finger," I warned. "You should call at five after."

"Nah. I'll call at noon."

"Why? You're giving her power over you."

He chuckled. "Have you checked her little finger lately?"

I chuckled too. Apparently, either getting email or something else had given him the ability to allow himself to love Mia. I'd been wrong when I thought she was more into him than he was into her.

"Well, don't let her wind you too tight there. One day, you might want to free yourself."

He laughed at that and we said our goodbyes since it was about a minute before noon, and he had that call to make.

At that moment, Grandma peeked her head into Mom's room.

"I'm sorry," she said. "I shouldn't have slapped you."

I was stunned. I honestly didn't think she had the ability to apologize to anyone, let alone her thirteen-year-old granddaughter.

My mom had always told me that if someone took the effort to apologize, I needed to accept the apology if it was sincere. She'd said that didn't mean I shouldn't remember what the person did, and she also said it didn't require me to say I was sorry either, especially if I had nothing to apologize for. For the first time, I had to force myself to accept, but not without something more.

"Okay. But never do that again."

She gave a single nod and closed the door. I heard her going downstairs again, this time not so loudly.

I lay there until I needed to get up to go to DQ. I needed to change clothes and grab some money from where I stashed my allowance each week. As I lay in my mom's bed, I thought about Grandma's apology. Had she meant it? She must have. I couldn't imagine her saying that just to make peace.

I also wondered why she hadn't waited for me to say I was sorry. Did she realize I had nothing to apologize for? Or had she thought I wouldn't do that even if I had something like that I needed to say? This made me wonder if her not waiting for me to apologize or even express some regret was a good thing or a bad one. Did she think I was incapable of thinking I was wrong? Or did she realize I'd not done anything wrong, really?

I wasn't sure what the answer was and didn't want to find out, at least not then. I had to get to DQ. The rain had stopped earlier than expected, and a hot fudge sundae was waiting for me to order it.

Once I met Cameron at DQ, I forgot all about what happened at my house. I even forgot my grandmother saying she was sorry she slapped me. I was having too much fun.

When I got back home, I took out my journal and wrote about what had happened that day with my grandmother. After writing about that, I wrote about the call with Nick, mostly because I thought it was funny how we'd talked about how he was wrapped around Mia's little finger.

I didn't mention how he'd joked about how he hadn't killed himself yet because I realized how silly it was of me to think he might have thought about it before. I mean, he was Nick, one of the nicest, best-looking guys at school.

8

When Mom got home that night, I didn't say anything about catching Grandma snooping in her room at first. I was waiting to see if Grandma would tell her. I definitely wanted to be there for that because I figured she would tell Mom why she was snooping. The problem was neither of us got around to saying anything because of an announcement from Mom.

After settling herself in with a glass of wine when she got home, she said she needed to talk to Grandma and me. I thought it would be something about trying to get along and, as she'd put it, "make amends." I wasn't looking forward to that, but it turned out to be even worse.

"I'll be attending a conference for nursery and landscape managers and owners in two weeks."

What? A conference? "You mean locally or out of town?"

"Out of town. San Diego, in fact."

I wanted to melt with a foreboding sense of doom. This wouldn't be some two-day thing. It was going to be four at the very least, considering the travel. Grandma was silent.

"How long will you be gone?"

"I leave a week from Friday and come back the following Tuesday."

"Why didn't you say something before?"

"Actually, I did, but I was placed on a waiting list. Apparently, someone canceled and my name came up. I got an email today."

"I don't remember you saying something," I protested as if that would keep her from attending.

"Well, I did. You must not have been paying attention."

Finally, Grandma spoke up, though her tone was not exactly happy. "Is this why you brought me here? To babysit?"

I resented the use of the word but couldn't complain, mostly because I was in shock.

"No, Mother. I was planning to have you keep Maureen at your place if I had been able to go. Either that or see if she could get a friend to let her stay there. Last resort could have been Jack and Jenny."

"Let me stay there! Please?!"

I saw Grandma's look, and while she probably hoped Mom would say yes, it also showed she was disappointed how much I wanted to stay anywhere but here with her.

Mom gave me the answer I knew she would but feared anyway. "No, Maureen. The most important reason I brought your grandmother here was to be sure someone was with her, if not during the school and work days, at least during the night."

I could feel myself deflate like a balloon that someone let the air out of in a matter of seconds. I looked at Grandma and felt both shame at my extreme need to be away from her as well as hurt that she looked as disappointed as I did.

"Look at it this way," Mom said. "It will give

you both some time to get to know each other more, which was the second most important reason I brought Grandma here."

"Against my will," Grandma said under her breath but loud enough to be heard.

"Mom," my mother said, "don't you think it's time you forgave me? And even if you don't, you need to stop taking it out on Maureen. It wasn't her fault."

I wasn't really sure what she was talking about, but it was obvious Grandma did. She set her jaw so hard it twitched and looked at me. "That's going to take some time."

I wasn't getting it. What was I being at least partially blamed for? Moving in with Mrs. Dawson? My mom running away with that guy to Jacksonville? I tried to think of his name and was surprised I couldn't, and Grandma had mentioned it just today. My mind reeled, though, with wondering what she thought was somehow my fault.

"What are you talking about?" I asked both of them. Turning to Grandma, I said, "What am I being blamed for that obviously isn't my fault?"

Grandma glanced at Mom, who said, "It's nothing, Maureen. That's the point."

I knew she was just putting me off, but I could tell that there was no way I would be told what they were referring to, at least not tonight. I began to wonder if Grandma would tell me, but right then it looked like she was planning to stay as tight-lipped as Mom about it.

I didn't know what it was, but it was painful to both of them to even remember it.

"I'm sorry if this inconveniences anyone, but it's going to happen whether or not you want it to. The two of you should make peace with each other. All of life will be easier if you do."

"What about you and Grandma?" I asked. "Don't you have to make peace, too?"

Mom looked down at her lap and said, "Yes. We do." Then looking at me, she said, "But I can tell you that doing so will be tougher for the two of us. Let's start with the easier mend first, and we'll go from there."

We all sat in silence for a moment before I asked if that was all and excused myself when my mom said it was.

Going to my bedroom, I lay in my bed and did my best to figure out what must have happened that I was being blamed for, even though it wasn't really my fault.

At first, the craziest ideas came to me. Had I been the one who shot my dad and Mom was just making up the story about the domestic disturbance call? Did Grandma once have a nice house and I burnt it down playing with matches? These were the only kinds of things I could come up with that would have created such anger. But then, if the first one had been true, Mom would have been angrier than Grandma. And if the second were true, Mom would probably have told me about it. As she'd mentioned, whatever it was wasn't my fault.

The reality was that no matter how much I thought about it, I wouldn't come up with the answer.

I took out my journal and wrote about what had

happened in the big discussion. It wasn't until I had nearly finished that I remembered that I hadn't told Mom about Grandma snooping through her stuff. I made a mental note to tell her tomorrow. I didn't want to talk to her right now.

I was about to put my journal away when someone knocked on my door. Thinking it was Mom, I said, "Come in." I figured since she was coming in my room, I would tell her about the snooping.

I was shocked to see Grandma's face peer around the door. "Can I come in?"

It was odd that this was probably the most civil thing she'd said to me since she arrived. Maybe in forever.

"Sure." I really didn't want her to come in for several reasons, not the least of them that I had my journal out with the words "Maureen's Private Journal—Keep Out!" written in large letters across the front sitting in my lap. I'd considered shoving it under my bed when she stuck her head in, but that would just be signaling her to snoop in my room next time.

I noticed her eyes fall on my journal before she looked back at my face.

"I'm sorry. The truth is there are a lot of things you don't know about me and my past as well as things about your mother you don't know. I'm afraid these things have influenced how I felt about you. I wanted to stop by here to say I will try to do better." She stood above me, apparently waiting for me to reply, but I couldn't think of anything much to say. Mostly, I was wondering what she meant by things I didn't know about her or my mom. What could those be? I'd always figured I knew pretty much everything since she'd told me about running off with that guy. I still couldn't remember his name, despite Grandma telling me what it was. But what could she have done that would be worse than that?

"What do I need to know about my mom?"

"Nothing. You don't need to know anything you don't already know. It's just that there's more to our relationship than you realize. Things that are private between just the two of us." She nodded toward my journal cover. "I can see you understand the idea of privacy."

I flipped the book over onto its cover and looked back at her. "If you understand that, why were you looking through Mom's stuff today?"

"I was looking for something that has to do with the problem between her and me. That's all you need to know." She hesitated before asking, "Why didn't you tell her about that?"

"I was waiting to see if you would tell her first. I thought you were Mom when you knocked on my door, and I was going to tell her when she came in."

"I don't suppose I can talk you out of doing that, could I?"

"Why should I keep it a secret?"

"Mostly because it will do more harm than good. If you want all of us to start getting along better, telling your mother I was going through her things would make that even more difficult than it is."

"But what were you looking for?"

"Telling you will also make it more difficult, I'm

afraid. Just understand that I was looking for something I felt it necessary to try to find. Believe it or not, I was doing that with your best interests at heart."

I didn't believe it, but I was willing to let what she had done stay a secret between the two of us, for now at least.

She thanked me when I told her I'd keep her snooping to myself provided she never did it again, but even I knew that only meant as long as I didn't catch her.

She left my room, closing the door behind her, leaving me to my thoughts. The maddening part was that what she had said haunted me. What if she really did have my best interests in mind? What in the world would my mother have in her room that somehow concerned me? And why would I be upset if I knew about it?

The idea that I might try to snoop myself made me blush with shame, but the temptation was strong. If it somehow concerned me, didn't I have a right to know what it was?

After dinner and watching TV, this time with Grandma joining us, I went to bed and lay awake for a long time, wondering if I should search my mom's bedroom myself.

As I drifted off, I suddenly remembered something my mother had told me once. She had warned me that the locked fireproof file box in her closet was off-limits until she died. She said it held her will and other important papers, but I should never open it until those things were needed.

Whatever Grandma was looking for was in there.

9

When I got to school the next day, I couldn't find Nick. He had always been in the same place in the cafeteria when I got there. His father dropped him off every day on his way to work, so he was always there before me. When I saw his usual seat was empty, I almost panicked.

Had his family disappeared again? What if he'd known they were probably leaving, and that's why Nick had told me about it—so I would know what happened?

I was so busy looking at the empty seat I didn't notice Mia sitting beside the chair. She looked as unhappy at Nick's absence as I felt.

I approached the table and Mia looked up at me. Before she could speak, I said, "Nick's not here!"

"Gee, I hadn't noticed," she said. Then she looked at me suspiciously and added, "Why are you upset about it?"

Great. She was worried I liked Nick after all.

"He just—" I wondered what I would say next. Should I tell her about his family's sudden tendency to leave town without notice? He'd told me that in confidence.

"Look, we're just friends, okay? I can miss a friend without him being my boyfriend."

Her look told me she only half-believed me. *There's something you're not telling me* was written all over her face, but I ignored it, allowing my explanation to stand.

I wanted to email him, but of course I couldn't do that until I got home, so I spent the rest of the day worrying that his family had moved somewhere and I would never see him again.

Thankfully, Cameron showed up at that moment, and although the conversation centered around Nick's absence at first, the focus moved away from me and how upset I was that Nick wasn't there.

Adding to my disappointment were thoughts of whatever it was my grandmother was searching for. She'd said she wouldn't do it again, but then what was stopping her? She was alone at the house every weekday. She could snoop anywhere she had a mind to.

Then I remembered she knew I had a journal. Would she search my room? True, she would have to stand on a chair to find it, but if she wanted to read it bad enough, she might do that.

I felt my cheeks blushing at the thought of that. I had some really personal stuff in there. And I mean *really* personal. Not just what boys I liked or anything. I mean the kind of personal stuff only I know about. The idea she might find my journal and read it made me feel sick.

I wanted to kick myself for not hiding it when she'd knocked and I thought it was my mom. I could have easily slipped it under a pillow, but I'd left it sitting in my lap like a ninny.

I spent the day worrying about Nick and my journal, waiting to be able to go home. When I finally got there, I found Grandma in the living room, watching TV. I tried to figure out from how she looked at me if she felt guilty about anything, but her face was mostly expressionless.

"How was your day?" she asked.

"Okay," I said, aware it was a lie as I went up to my room.

Logging into my computer, I opened my email. I held my breath when I saw Nick had emailed me that morning. Was he saying goodbye?

I clicked on it and read.

Hey, Maureen. It's Nick. I just wanted to let you know I'm not feeling well today and stayed home. I didn't want you thinking we'd left town suddenly. I should be in school tomorrow. My mom thinks it's just a 24 hour thing. I hope she's right. I hate throwing up.

Later,

Nick

Relieved, I relaxed a bit concerning Nick. He'd just been home sick, like any kid. What did it say about me that I jumped to the worst conclusion before thinking something simple like he might not feel well? I thought about that for a moment. It's sad that people are that way, always thinking the worst. Then again, he'd known I might worry, which was why he sent the email in the first place.

I reread it and almost laughed at the sentence "It's Nick" as if I wouldn't already know that from the email address. I laughed again, feeling the relief of laughter to help ease my mind.

Then I began worrying about my journal and my

snoopy grandmother being here all day. Her reaction when I came home suggested maybe she hadn't found it, but I couldn't be sure.

I grabbed the chair and went to my closet. Climbing up, I reached for my journal. It was where I'd left it, but I still couldn't be sure she hadn't touched it. I decided to booby trap it so I would know if she ever did.

I took three pennies from my drawer where I kept some spare change and stacked them on top of each other on the journal. They were just out of sight of someone who might take it down but close enough for me to be able to touch them to verify they were still in a stack. If Grandma took my journal down from the closet shelf, the pennies would fall, and she'd know I had placed them there to make sure nobody read it. She would probably just put the pennies back on the journal. She might even stack them, but I had the pennies in order of date with the oldest one on the bottom.

I smiled at my cleverness and sat back down at my desk to do my homework.

When I had finished, I went downstairs to get something to drink. Grandma heard me and called me into the living room and turned off the TV. She motioned for me to sit in a chair facing her.

"I've been thinking about something."

"What?"

"Well…us."

"What about us?"

She took a deep breath and said, "Your mom is right. We need to get to know each other better. Perhaps if we did, we'd like and understand each other more."

Her words kind of shocked me. Basically, she was admitting she didn't like me. At least that's what I heard.

"I admit I tend to push people away, but I have my reasons," she said.

"What reasons?"

She looked at me for so long I thought she wasn't going to say anything and that the conversation was over before it began.

"Maybe I'll tell you in time. Suffice it to say I've been hurt badly in my life, and it affects how I treat others." She looked at her lap. "I don't want you to be the same way when you grow up."

I considered telling her how many times she had hurt me already but didn't. As Mom would say, that wouldn't help anything. I wanted this conversation to continue if for no other reason than I was curious. How badly could someone have treated her that she pushed people away, including her own granddaughter?

I figured she was waiting for me to respond, so I said, "I don't want to be like that either." That was true. I couldn't imagine a worse life than constantly pushing people away because I had been hurt by someone. That would make life so...lonely.

"I'm glad. So, what do you say? Ready to get to know me better and let me get to know you?"

The thought of my journal flashed through my mind again, and I wondered if this was about her confessing to reading it. She would have gotten to know me *a lot* if she'd done that. Too much, really.

"Can I ask you a question?"

"You can ask, but I don't guarantee I'll answer."

That was fair enough. That would allow me to refuse to answer a question of hers that made me uncomfortable.

"What were you looking for in Mom's bedroom?"

"That's something I can't tell you right now, but just know it's something important. Something I feel you should see as well."

That was weird. She was searching for something she thought I needed to see? Why wouldn't Mom show it to me if I needed to see it?

"You mean I've not seen it?"

"No, but one day I think you should. In fact, I'm certain you will one day, whether or not I ever find it. Your mother will probably show it to you."

"So Mom has kept me from seeing this...whatever it is?"

"Yes, and she has her reasons, but I think it's about time you...well...saw it."

I was beyond puzzled. What in the world was she talking about?

"Does it involve me?"

She thought before answering. "Yes."

"Then why hasn't Mom shown it to me?"

"Because she doesn't want to hurt you."

Okay, this was getting too weird. "Why would it hurt me?"

"I can't tell you that, but it would. I don't think you'd be devastated or anything like that, but it's something I think you should know that your mom believes should wait another year or two."

"Do you want to show it to me to hurt me?"

"No. I just believe it's time for you to know. The truth is it involves me, your mother, and you."

"Why won't you just tell me if you think I should know?"

"Because you wouldn't believe me without the proof."

"Did my mother do something terrible she's not telling me about? Something that involves me?" I couldn't imagine what it would be.

"I can't answer that, really. You already know about the young man she ran off with and killed."

That thought, that she had told me about that but not whatever it was my grandma was talking about, made me wonder how terrible whatever she wasn't telling me could be.

"How does it involve you?" I asked.

"It just does." She heaved another big sigh and said, "This isn't what I wanted to talk about. Mostly I wanted to talk about my past to let you know I'm not the mean person you think I am."

I asked several more questions about whatever it was she and Mom were hiding from me, but she refused to discuss it anymore.

"I'll just ask Mom, then," I finally said.

"She won't tell you. At least not yet. And asking her would just cause more problems and solve none."

"How's that?"

"She'd know I've told you there's something you don't know about your mother's and my past. She would also know exactly what that was, and that would just increase the tension in an already tense home."

"But—"

"How about this? I talk to your mom again about this and see if she's willing to tell you our family secret."

Family secret? Was that what this was? "Am I adopted or something?"

She gave me a shocked look. "No. Your mother did not adopt you. Just hold off and relax. I'll talk to her and see if I can talk her into showing you what I was looking for."

I decided to ask her something else that was related to that. "Have you searched for it again? You were here all day alone. You could have, you know."

"No, I didn't. I told you I wouldn't, and I kept my word."

Well, that was something, at least. If she was willing to keep a promise to me, maybe the relationship was salvageable. I hesitated to ask the next question.

"Did you try to find my journal?" I was angry at myself because I could feel my cheeks blushing a bright red.

"Of course not. A girl's journal is a private thing. I was young once myself, you know, and I can imagine how furious you would be if anyone read it. To be honest, though, I doubt anything you say in there would surprise me very much."

I wasn't sure about that, but I let it drop before she started asking me what I might have put in there that I thought would surprise her.

"What did you want to tell me about your past?" I finally asked.

"My mother was quite the character. Did you know that?"

"No. What do you mean, a character?"

"She had a marvelous sense of humor and loved playing harmless practical jokes on people, for one thing."

I was shocked. A woman with a "marvelous sense of humor" raised this woman who never seemed to laugh at anything? Had it skipped a generation or something? Then I thought about my mom and figured maybe it skipped two. She had a good sense of humor, but I wouldn't call it "marvelous." Then again, I wouldn't say mine was all that marvelous either. That made me wonder if maybe Grandma was adopted but didn't know it.

"What kind of practical jokes?" I admit I was curious.

"One time, she dressed up like a man, even putting on a man's hat to hide her hair, and used an eyebrow pencil to paint on a thin mustache. We had these neighbors, two spinsters who couldn't see very well and refused to wear glasses because they were too vain. Mama got my sister, Jean, to dress up all frumpy and then sent me to visit the sisters.

"About five minutes after I arrived, the doorbell rang. Ida, one of the neighbors, got up to answer it, and in walks my mother and Jean, who was wearing a wide-brimmed hat to help hide her face."

I couldn't help it. I started laughing at the mental image of a woman dressed up like a man and pulling a harmless joke like this. Grandma smiled at me. I suppose it wasn't the first time she'd smiled at me, but I couldn't remember her doing it before.

She continued with the story. "Anyway, I could tell Jean was about to bust from laughing. Her shoulders were sort of bouncing from her efforts to hold it in.

"Mama, in this deep voice, said, "Sorry to bother you ladies, but my car broke down about a block from here, and this is the first house to answer the door. May I use your phone to call someone?"

"You mean she actually called a mechanic?" I asked.

"No. She dialed our number. She'd told my father about what we were doing, so he just answered the phone and laughed at my mother's antics. And remember, this was before cell phones, so people only had tabletop or wall hanging phones with a numbered wheel you spun with your finger to dial.

"Anyway, she pretended to be speaking to a mechanic, though it was really my dad. Then she hung up and said they would be there in about a half hour."

"What did y'all do for thirty minutes?"

"My mother proceeded to make up a long, complicated story about how they were from out of town and were on their way to visit his wife's sister, who lived about a hundred miles from there. She even told them his wife was mute and couldn't hear or speak to explain why she wasn't saying anything. It was quite a performance."

"Did they figure it out?"

"No. Finally, Mama said, 'Don't you recognize me?' and they shook their heads, asking when they'd met before. Mama reached up and took off the hat she was wearing, and Jean, released from having to hold in the laughter, nearly wet her pants giggling about it.

One of the sisters cackled she was so surprised. She thought it was hilarious. The other sister, not so much. She thought it was terrible to play a trick on them. The sister who thought it was funny said, "Oh, get over it, Betsy. It didn't hurt anyone."

"Your mother really did that?" I asked, still trying to picture Grandma having such a childhood.

"Yes, and even more. Like I said, she was quite a character."

Finally, I couldn't hold in what I was thinking any longer. "Grandma, if you grew up with a mother like that, why are you so—" I decided to let her fill in the insulting word.

"Dour?" she suggested.

"I guess."

"I had a happy childhood. Unfortunately, that doesn't guarantee a happy adulthood."

"What happened?"

"Later," she said. "Right now, I want you to know I've not always been so angry at life."

With that, she got up and went to the kitchen. I watched her go and realized that if my life hadn't been as good as it had, I might be 'dour' too. Maybe I needed to give my grandmother some slack, but she needed to give me some, too. She also needed to solve the mystery that was growing in my mind.

When Mom got home from work, I wanted to ask about what Grandma had told me about whatever it was she'd been searching for in my mother's room. I knew where it was, and it's possible Grandma had found the locked fireproof box and knew, too. Neither of us could get into it, though.

But of course, Mom could. She had the key, but where was it?

10

Nick sat at the family's computer. This was the best part of staying home sick: nobody to bother him when he was on the family's only computer. He'd been forced to use the public library's computer to send Ray an email, but with nobody else home, he had the computer to himself. He just needed to make sure he remembered to delete the visit to Gmail in the history. He wanted to check to see if he had a reply from Ray and email Maureen about why he was absent. He suspected she might freak out if he didn't show for school after what he'd told her.

Opening his email, he saw he had a reply from Ray. He knew if he opened it first, he might not email Maureen, so he did that first. When he'd finished with that, he read the email from Ray. As he did, a sense of dread came over him.

Dude!

Great to hear from you...FINALLY!! You know I was totally bummed when you called to tell me you were moving but you didn't know where. I figured you'd at least call when you got where you were going, but all I got was crickets. At first, I wondered why all the secrecy, but then some dudes came by and asked if I knew where you'd gone. I was playing catch with Pete in my front yard, and they stopped on the street. They didn't have badges or anything, and they could have been cops, but when I asked if they were, they said no. They coulda been lying, but why would they? Anyways, I told them I had no idea where you were. They looked like they didn't believe me, and one of them says to me, all menacing like, "Are you lying to us?" It kinda scared me. They definitely looked real serious. I asked why they were looking for you, but they said they were looking for your dad. They didn't say anything else about why they wanted to find him, but I figured it had something to do with why you guys left in such a hurry. I have to admit I'm scared for you and your family. These dudes looked like they could punch their way through a concrete wall! I don't want to scare you or anything, but I figured you should know. I'd have told you before now, but I had no idea how to contact you. Anyways, I'm glad you finally got in touch. I emailed your old email, but it came back that the account was closed. That freaked me out too. I don't know what's going on, but you guys need to lay low for a while. I even deleted your email. Someone could hack it and find you. Anyways, it's great to hear from you. Email back when you can.

L8r!

Ray

Someone had gone so far as to stop and ask Ray about him? This was not good. Not at all. Why ask about him? Was someone trying to kill them? What had his father done to make these people want to find them? And what would they do if they succeeded?

Suddenly, Nick felt like maybe he shouldn't have emailed Ray in the first place. What if they did hack his email? Nick had no idea how that was done, but he knew it was possible. Maybe easy for someone who knew what they were doing.

He wondered if he should tell his parents what he'd done. After a few minutes, though, he decided he was overreacting, as usual. Who would hack some kid's email? Besides, he'd emailed Ray a couple of days ago, and nobody had shown up at their door. A flight would only take a few hours.

He decided he'd dodged a bullet—maybe literally—and figured any future emails to Ray that mentioned where they were would be in a code they had worked out a couple of years ago. They had made up a code based on the periodic table of elements. Each letter was represented by numbers. For example, the letter E, the most common letter in English, could be many different number combinations, like 22 for helium. The first number was the atomic number for the element, the second number was the placement. A 21 would be an H because the first letter in the helium's abbreviation was H. Likewise, 262 would also be an E, since the second letter in the abbreviation for iron, the twenty-sixth element, was also an E. The only letters not in the table were J and Q. For those, they would use the number 0 for the first number since no element had zero for its atomic number, and it would be easy to figure out which letter they meant.

The best thing about it was he and Ray didn't have to carry some sort of code translator. The periodic table was accessible on the internet. They were proud of themselves for creating such an easy code that would be nearly impossible to decipher if you didn't know its rules.

He replied to Ray, using the code when he talked about Denton. Mostly, he told Ray how happy he was to get a reply.

Erasing the computer's history and shutting it down, Nick lay down on his bed. He tried to get Ray's email off his mind, but it wouldn't leave him alone. For now, he would stick with his decision not to tell his folks. But at the same time, he prayed he was making the right choice.

Osbourne's flight landed in Atlanta, the first leg of his journey to a small town called Denton on Florida's northern Gulf Coast. Nearly every flight to the Southeast went through Atlanta. His next flight would take him to Wharton, and from there he would rent a car and drive the short distance to Denton.

Once there, he would pay for the prearranged hotel room on the beach. No sense in wasting a trip to Florida, after all. A package was waiting for him at the hotel because carrying a gun on a plane was nearly impossible, and even if he could figure a way to accomplish that, he wouldn't. Discovery was too likely, with the results too dangerous to his freedom.

He would then do his best to find out where the Winslows lived in Denton. That wouldn't take long. He had a plan for how to accomplish that, and once he knew where they were, the rest would be as simple as a knock on the door late at night. Late-night knocks were always answered by the man of the house. Two seconds after opening the door,

Winslow would no longer be a problem. The biggest question was if he would be forced to take care of the wife and kids after that. It would be easy, but he would avoid it if possible. If they saw nothing, they would live. If they could identify him? That would be a different story. He would do what he had to.

It's why they paid him. He'd been paid only to kill Winslow. Anyone else was up to him to protect himself and his employers. It was that simple and that ugly.

Taking down the only bag he had from the overhead bin, Osbourne made his way down the loading ramp to the terminal. His next flight wasn't for two hours, so he went to an airport bar for a scotch.

"What'll you have?" the bartender asked.

"Johnny Walker Red on the rocks." He preferred the blue label, but airport bars didn't keep that in stock due to the price.

As he sat sipping his scotch, he waited for his plane to be announced. He was happy with his solitude in the multitude, but a man sitting beside him felt the need to start a conversation.

"So where you headed?" he asked as he downed the rest of his drink and motioned for the bartender to refill it.

"Nowhere special." Osbourne hoped his laconic answer would urge the man to choose another ten-minute friend.

"That's no fun! Me? I'm—"

Osbourne turned to the man, cutting off his words. "No offense, but I'm not in the mood for chitchat." Osbourne's expression said more than his words.

The man's smile faded quickly. "Sorry," he said and turned toward the bartender, who was setting his fresh drink on the bar.

Osbourne rose and went to a seat at a table that a couple had just vacated and ignored the rest of the travelers as best he could. A man who did what he did for a living needed to be a loner by necessity.

Mr. Chatty turned to a woman who sat down in the seat Osbourne had vacated. "How you doin', Darlin'?"

Osbourne had to smile as Chatty's smile once again faded. She obviously wasn't in the mood for chitchat either.

His flight was finally called and Osbourne rose from the table and made his way to the nearby gate. When he noticed Mr. Chatty boarding with the other first class passengers on the same flight, Osbourne frowned. When Chatty sat in the seat beside Osbourne, he wanted to lure the man into the washroom and kill him.

Sure enough, the man turned to him as they sat. "Well, you might not be in the mood for chitchat, but it's interesting we're not only on the same flight to Wharton but seated next to each other. Is that kismet or not?"

Osbourne leaned close to the man to make sure nobody overheard what he would say. "It's not kismet. It's bad luck. My bad luck. As I told you, I am not interested in whatever you have to say. Don't speak to me again."

Chatty held up a hand. "Easy, man. I don't

have to get whacked over the head. I get it. Won't say another word to you. Promise. But, dude, you need to lighten up. It's just conversation."

"From now on, it will be conversation that doesn't involve me." Osbourne leaned back into his seat and buckled the seatbelt, doing his best to ignore Mr. Chatty.

Chatty, however, turned to the passenger in the seat across the aisle and struck up a conversation. This person, a man who looked to be in his sixties, was apparently fine with chitchat. Osbourne had to listen to them prattling the entire flight to Wharton.

When the plane landed, Osbourne couldn't extract himself fast enough. He nearly shoved Mr. Chatty out of his way and muscled his bag from the bin. Hurrying from the plane, he made it to car rental and within twenty minutes of deboarding was in a comfortable car speeding toward Denton and his target.

Later, upon entering the beachfront hotel, he received the package he'd mailed himself and went up to his room. After showering and changing, he stepped out of the room and made his way to the hotel's restaurant attached to the lobby.

He was at his table when he overheard the voice of Mr. Chatty.

Okay, he thought, *this is too much of a coincidence.* Maybe it was his natural paranoia, or perhaps it was real, but Osbourne couldn't shake the feeling he was being tailed. He didn't recall seeing Mr. Chatty on the plane from San Fran, but that didn't mean he wasn't on it. That flight was on an Airbus A380, a jumbo jet, so it would be easy not to notice the man among more than 500 passengers.

He decided he couldn't take the chance. Chatty had to die, even if this was all a coincidence, which Osbourne was beginning to doubt. Maybe he was a Fed. Or perhaps he worked for someone who had hired him to kill Osbourne. He'd made enough enemies in his life to warrant that.

After finishing his meal, he went to the table where Chatty was sitting with a woman.

"I want to apologize," Osbourne said. "Long day."

"Think nothing of it," Chatty said, extending his hand to shake.

Osbourne took it out of necessity and offered another apology and excused himself.

"Probably see you around!" Chatty said after the retreating Osbourne.

"You can count on it," Osbourne said and returned to his room to begin taking care of the reason he'd come here in the first place.

11

I spotted Nick when I arrived at school the next day. He looked a bit haggard, as if he still felt ill. Walking up, I sat across the cafeteria table from him.

"You okay?" I asked.

Looking up, he said, "Yeah."

"You don't sound like it, and you don't look like it either."

"I didn't sleep much last night."

"Still feeling sick?"

He looked at me, and I could see the lie coming. "Yeah."

As I got older, I found I was getting more like my mother. She could see a lie coming before I drew a breath to tell it. Now, I wasn't sure why Nick couldn't sleep last night, but it wasn't because he was still feeling sick, if indeed he ever had. Was he just ditching school because—because of what?

I decided to find out. I had once asked my mother to describe me in one word. Mom had said *stubborn* immediately without even thinking about it.

"Nick?"

"Yeah?"

"Are we friends?"

"Sure."

"Good friends?"

"I guess."

"Do you trust me?"

"You know I do."

"Then why won't you tell me why you couldn't sleep last night?"

"I told you. I was still feeling sick."

"That's what you said, but it's not true."

"And how would you know that? Do you have some kind of camera set up to watch me 24/7?"

"Of course not."

"Then how would you know I wasn't feeling sick? Why don't you believe me?"

I didn't really know why, but I didn't, and I knew I was right. It was something in his look when he said it, like a hope that I would believe him.

"Let's just say I could tell. It was kinda obvious."

He took a deep breath and let it out slowly, as if calming his temper. I wondered if I'd gone too far.

"You swear you won't tell anyone? I mean nobody, not even your cat."

"I don't have a cat."

"I don't care. I just need you to understand how important it is you say nothing to anyone if I tell you."

I crossed my heart with my index finger of my right hand. "May maggots start eating me an hour before I die if I tell."

Nick looked around as if checking for eavesdroppers. Nobody was paying us any attention. Taking another breath, he leaned closer. "It's because—"

"Hey, Nicky!" It was Mia. She was making a

beeline to us from my left. When she said that, I nearly jumped out of my skin.

Sitting next to Nick as closely as she could, Mia hooked her arm through his and looked daggers at me. "So, what are y'all talking about?"

I had to think of something and think of it fast. Mia's eyes were almost green she was so jealous of our time together.

Stalling, I looked around and said, "I'll tell you later."

Nick glared at me but couldn't say anything without giving it away that our conversation was private. Realizing how my reply had sounded I said, "Okay, I'll tell you now. Nick was about to ask me about something he was planning to get you for your birthday."

"Really?!" Mia squealed, pulling herself closer to Nick, if that was possible and grinning at him. "But my birthday's not for another two months!"

"Gotta plan early and save up," he said to Mia while staring at me.

I looked at Mia and said, "So, if you'll leave us alone for a few minutes, maybe I can help him decide if what he's thinking of getting you is something you'll want."

Mia glanced around and pointed at an empty table about thirty feet away. "Okay, but I won't go far. I'll sit over there and when you're done, just signal me." Rising, she strode over to the table and sat down, keeping her gaze and grin on Nick.

Nick leaned closer. "I thought you were going to tell her what we were really talking about."

"I wouldn't do that. I like Mia, but trusting her

with anything she could tell someone else is not a good idea."

"Thanks for getting us out of that. She's really insecure about stuff."

"Yeah, I know. Now, why did you have trouble sleeping last night?"

He took another deep breath and said, "I got an email from my friend Ray back in California. He told me some people had asked him about where we had moved. Guys who said they weren't cops. It probably has something to do with why my dad is so secretive about where we are."

I did my best to keep a straight face and not give away that Nick had dropped this bombshell. Mia was surely watching my face to see my reaction to her "gift."

"What do you think about that?" Nick asked. "Do you think I'm right? That my dad is running from someone?"

"I hate to say it, but yeah. Did your friend tell you anything else about them?"

"No, only that they were looking for me. Well, not me. They told Ray they were looking for my dad and wanted to know where we'd moved."

"Jeez. Did you tell your parents?"

"No. You think I should? I'll get in trouble for emailing Ray, and since he didn't know where we'd gone, he couldn't tell them anything. It's not like they'll come back and ask again. I mean, we're no worse off than we were before. On the run with nobody knowing where we disappeared to."

"These guys sound dangerous," I said.

Nick leaned back. "I know."

"We'll talk more in English class," I said and signaled for Mia to return. Leaving her there for too long would make her wonder if I had told the truth. I hadn't, of course, and now we were going to have to come up with a great birthday gift for Mia.

"So? Will I like it?" she asked me as she sat.

"Of course," I said. Then looking directly at her, I added, "And Mia?"

"Yeah?"

"Nick and I are just friends. That and nothing more. Always will be nothing more. I'm not interested in him like that, and he's not interested in me."

"I'm not jealous of you two!" she said, doing her best to sound sincere.

"Could have fooled me," I said. "And if you keep thinking Nick and I have something going that you wouldn't like, I'll tell him about this summer at the lake house."

Mia blushed about ten shades of red. "You wouldn't!"

"Just get over your jealousies, and I won't," I said. Then grabbing my bookbag, I stood to leave just as Cameron was arriving.

"The lake house?" Nick said.

"It's nothing!" Mia answered.

"What's up?" Cameron asked, acknowledging the tension in Mia's tone.

"Nothing," I said. "Mia just needs to figure out Nick and I aren't wanting a romance with each other."

Cameron laughed and looked at Mia. "Jeez, girl! I can assure you that ain't gonna happen!"

Mia was still red when I left. Whether from my threat to tell what had happened that summer or because she felt ashamed of being jealous, I don't know, but I hoped whatever it was would make her see that I had no designs on Nick, and he had none on me.

The lake house story was only mildly embarrassing, but I knew she wouldn't want Nick to know about it. My mom had allowed me to go with Mia for a week to stay at a house her family owned at a lake in central Alabama. One day her parents were in town getting some groceries and other things and left the two of us there. Mia had asked me if I'd ever been skinny-dipping. When I told her I hadn't, she acted like I was saying I had never eaten ice cream or something. Next thing you know, she's buck naked and jumping into the lake off the small pier they had behind the house. It had taken her ten minutes to convince me to try it, but I jumped in first before taking off my swimsuit to make sure nobody else could see me. I was convinced some boys were watching us with binoculars or something.

Anyway, we swam around for another ten minutes before getting out. Before we did, she managed to get my swimsuit away from me and forced me to get out of the water with nothing on so I could get back into it.

She wasn't embarrassed that someone might see her at all. She was strutting around on the dock with nothing on, holding out my swimsuit, saying "Here it is! Come get it!" Then she yelled really loud so anyone could hear, "You can't stay naked in the water all day, you know!" I'd been mad the rest of the day before forgiving her. But that was just Mia. She could really make me mad sometimes. It was kind of funny though. She didn't seem to mind if someone saw her naked at the lake, but she definitely didn't want Nick to know about it. But I had always known there was a wild streak in Mia a mile wide. Sometimes, I thought she might do crazy things that could get her in trouble just for the thrill of it.

In English class, Nick and I talked again about what had happened in California. I was like Nick. On the one hand, I wanted him to tell his folks, but on the other, I felt these possibly bad people still knew nothing. Nick's family had moved clear across the country, and nobody had shown up since the email to Ray. How could they find Nick's family? I convinced myself we were worrying about nothing.

12

The Friday arrived when my mom was flying to San Diego for her conference. I'll be honest and say I didn't make her leaving easy. I was angry all day, hoping that my anger might make her decide never to do this again. Grandma and I were getting along better. She'd told me a few more stories from her childhood, and that helped me get to know her better, but I still wasn't looking forward to being alone with her until the following Tuesday.

One of her employees picked her up to take her to the airport. Mom left the house early enough that I saw her off before having to go to school, but too late to catch the bus. Grandma was given the duty to drive me, and neither of us spoke much until I asked her if she planned to go searching for whatever mysterious thing she was looking for in Mom's room. I probably did that because I was in a foul mood. She'd already told me she wouldn't do that again, but I didn't really trust her. After all, I was curious about what she had been looking for enough to consider trying to get into Mom's locked file box and see if it was there.

When I asked if she planned to keep searching, she said, "I told you I wouldn't."

Her answer sounded like more of an evasion than anything. I would have preferred an outright answer that no, she wouldn't search for it. This led me to ask, "Why won't you tell me what it is that you're so all-fired determined to find?"

Glancing at me then back at the road, she said, "You want me to find it, don't you?"

"Why would I want that?"

"So you could find out what it is that I'm, as you put it, 'so all-fired determined to find,' right?"

"Would you tell me what it is if you did find it?"

"That's exactly why I want to find it. You'll need proof that what I'm telling you is true."

"Is it about another story about your mom and your childhood?"

"No, but it's a story you need to know eventually." We had arrived at school. She turned to me and said, "It will explain a lot, but it won't be pleasant for you. Your mother doesn't think you should know about it, but I think you should."

"It's not right for you to do what you're doing," I said, ignoring that she'd said she wouldn't continue searching because we both knew better.

"Maybe not, but I can't rest peacefully until I know that you know what the document I'm searching for says concerning you." She paused. "You have a right to know it."

"If I have a right to know it, why doesn't Mom tell me?"

"Because it's a painful thing, and we sometimes do everything we can not to think of those things that cause us or our loved ones pain."

I needed to get out and start my school day, but I needed the answer to one more question. "Is it painful for you, too?"

When she looked at me, her eyes were brimming. I was startled to see she was so close to crying. "Yes. Very painful."

"Then why do you think about it?"

"Because I can't help it. It's part of who I am."

Confusion, curiosity, unexpected compassion, and fear washed over me. I felt my own eyes well up. I thought about telling Grandma about the file box hidden in Mom's room. I knew where it was, and it was possible she hadn't found it when she'd been looking before. Still, I had no idea where the key might be, so I said nothing except goodbye and climbed out of the car.

I spent most of the day wondering what might be so painful that Grandma would cry just from thinking about it, and it scared me that it somehow involved me. Was I destined to die young from some disease? That sounded crazy, but I couldn't come up with anything that involved me that could be so painful.

When I got home that day, Grandma was taking a nap. I didn't disturb her. Instead, I went into my mother's room. Because important papers and an amount of cash were in the locked, fireproof box, and Mom didn't want a burglar to find it, she'd hidden the box behind a heavy chest-of-drawers in the back of her walk-in closet. She kept some lingerie and other intimate apparel in the chest. Anyone looking would assume nothing was behind it. The chest was about six inches from the wall, and clothes hung along each side to sort of hide that there was even a small gap. Burglars would assume there was nothing there, as would Grandma.

Mom had said the file box was locked, but I hoped maybe she'd forgotten to lock it the last time she'd opened it. It was a long shot but at least worth the look.

I managed to scoot the chest-of-drawers out from the wall enough to shimmy along one side of it and retrieve the file box from behind it. When I did this, I saw a small key taped to the back of the chest.

My breathing stopped. It had to be the key to the box. Why else put it right where the box sat? Mom had told me about the file box but not the key.

When I pulled on the tape, some of the finish on the back of the chest-of-drawers came with it. The key had been there a long time. A year or more, at least. The tape itself was yellowed with age, and I knew that Mom would be able to tell it had been removed if she ever had to get into the file box. I couldn't help that now. It wasn't as if I could replace the key with the same piece of tape. I'd have to cross that bridge when I got to it, which would most certainly happen one day.

Lifting the box and taking the key with me, I placed the file box on Mom's bed. My hands shook so much as I tried to insert the key that it took me a few tries to line everything up.

When the key was in place, I turned the lock carefully in case it wasn't the right key. It wouldn't do to break a key off in the lock.

The lock turned. I held my breath. Hands shaking, I lifted the lid and peered inside.

I'm not sure what I expected to see, but nothing

inside seemed in the least bit ominous. About a dozen file folders stood in the box, each holding anywhere from a few pieces of paper to maybe a dozen. Searching through each wouldn't take long, but the thought of Grandma catching me doing exactly what I'd been angry at her for doing made me rush. I also saw a business-size letter envelope behind the folders that I knew would hold the emergency cash. Mom had already told me there was a thousand dollars in twenties in there. I left the envelope alone.

Being careful to keep the folders in the same order, I pulled one file at a time and searched the contents, replacing each folder as I finished.

Several folders were about finances. Bank information, old tax forms, mortgage information on the house, and the legal documents for her business were stacked inside several of the folders. In another folder I found Mom's and my birth certificates, my parents' marriage license, my father's death certificate, and other things I considered to be about family.

I returned that folder and continued going through each one until I was finished. Now, I was puzzled. There hadn't been a single thing in there that concerned me. If what Grandma was so determined to find wasn't in here, where was it? Most of this was just boring stuff. Actually, all of it was. Grandma had suggested there was some secret that involved me that she felt I had a right to know.

I looked at the file box and shook my head. I'd gone to all this trouble, and I'd be in trouble eventually for going into the box in the first place, and now I had nothing to show for it. Nothing was in there that concerned me at all.

As I closed the box and locked it to return it to its place, a thought struck me.

Actually, there had been something that concerned me in that box, but how it would reveal some sort of secret my mom was keeping from me, I had no idea.

My birth certificate. That concerned me. Did it reveal my parents weren't married yet when she had me? I suppose that could be the big secret, but really, why would it matter? This wasn't the 19th century, and I was fairly certain my mom and dad would have slept together before getting married. My mom had never been an angel when it came to stuff like that. After all, she'd run away with a guy whose name was not spoken when she was fifteen.

Or had she lied about her age when she'd done that, and this devil she'd been with was my father? But what proof would be on a birth certificate for something like that?

Curious beyond measure, I opened the file box again and found the folder with what I had considered "family stuff" and pulled it out.

With trembling hands, I opened the folder and found my birth certificate. I began to read it. My name, Maureen Shaw was the first thing I noticed. Shaw? That was my mom's maiden name! What about Lindstrom? Then that must be it. I was born before my parents were married, and they'd changed my last name after the wedding.

Again, I wondered why that would be such a secret. Lots of kids were born out of wedlock these days. Some people decided never to marry each other, just live as a family anyway. Could this really be the big, dark secret? And why would Grandma be so upset by this? It wasn't as if Mom had been this virginal person when she was growing up. I mean, mistakes happen, even for women on the pill.

I continued reading my birth certificate, looking for anything out of the ordinary beyond my last name—along with NMN in the area labeled "CHILD'S MIDDLE NAME." I knew that meant "no middle name." That was different too, since while I hated my middle name, I did have one. They must have given me one when they changed my last name.

I saw my birth weight – 7 lbs. 8 oz. The date and time of birth, the date matching my birthday and year. Apparently, I was born at 2:47 a.m. My length, 18 and 3/4 inches. Mother's name, Brandy Shaw (not Lindstrom). Father's name.

I froze, my eyes shooting open with shock.

Jeff Borden.

I'd heard that name before. Where had I heard it? Then it hit me. And it hit me hard.

Jeff Borden was my mother's stepfather, the man Grandma had moved herself, Mom, and Uncle Ryan to Florida to be with. A man I knew Mom detested almost as much as the guy she'd run away with.

The words on the certificate blurred as tears filled my eyes. This had to be it. Mom had slept with her stepfather? It didn't seem real, but here it was, printed on a legal document I could no longer see.

Mom had hated the man! Why would she have sex with him? I was so confused and busy crying, sobbing apparently, that I didn't notice my grandmother until she was standing beside me and spoke.

"I see you found it," she said.

Startled, I whipped around and looked up at her. That was when I noticed how loud I was sobbing. The sound seemed to come from somewhere else, as if I wasn't the one crying, but someone seated near me was.

I wanted to run. To hide and never come out again. For some reason, shame filled me, as if I had been the one to have sex with my stepfather. It felt as though my grandmother hadn't found me snooping where I'd forbidden her to snoop but had caught me in the middle of very forbidden sex.

As I stood to run, though, she caught me and held me against her in what I believe was the first real hug she'd ever given me.

I buried my face into her, sobbing. I could still hear the sounds, but now they sounded distant and muffled. Then her voice pierced my cries.

"It's okay, sweetheart. Let it out. It's okay."

After a few minutes, my sobs began to quiet and I managed to get control of myself. I still leaned into her, savoring the warmth of a hug I only then realized how much I'd wanted my entire life. I could hear the gurgling noises her belly made as I pressed the side of my face to her, and for some reason, that soothed me.

"Why?" I asked. It was all I could think to say.

"Why didn't she tell you?"

"That, but more. Why did she sleep with him? She hated him."

"Oh, sweetheart. She didn't sleep with him. He raped her."

I felt my scalp prickle at the words. Rape? My mother had been raped by her stepfather?

"Why didn't she get an abortion?" An odd feeling washed over me as I said it. It was eerie talking about aborting me, but at the same time, I would have understood if she had.

"He wouldn't allow it. I had to have a hysterectomy, so I couldn't have any more children. Jeff wanted a child of his own, so he forced your mother to carry the baby to full term. Once you were born, I realized I'd had enough of him. I divorced him. He died in a car accident two weeks after the divorce was final. Otherwise, I would have moved back to North Carolina, even though I loved it here. Still do, in fact."

"Does Mom resent me?" I'd heard women often resented children born from rape.

"No, dear. She hated what he did to her, but she loves you. Always has from the moment you took your first breath. She'd intended to put you up for adoption, but she couldn't once she held you. As she told me at the time, 'It's not her fault, so I can't give her up.' Sometimes women can't stand the child they have in those circumstances. Not your mom."

"So my dad isn't my dad?"

"No, dear."

Great. My real father is a rapist, not a decorated police officer, I thought. "I feel...dirty," I said.

Grandma sat on Mom's bed, pulling me into her lap. Again, I realized how long I'd wanted that.

"You mustn't feel that way."

I breathed in her smell, a slight fragrance of lilac, and considered how I'd felt when she hugged me and again when she pulled me into her lap. I understood then that I'd never hated her exactly. I loved her and just wanted her to love me back.

"Grandma?"

"Yes?"

"I love you."

I felt her arms tighten around me, holding me as close as she could. "I love you, too," she said, but her voice sounded strained.

13

I spent the evening talking to Grandma like I'd never talked to her before. I don't mean I cussed or anything. I just was honest with her and asked as much as I could about the man who was my real father, at least biologically. She told me that he wasn't a good person (I knew that), and that I really didn't look anything like him, which got me to thinking.

"Is there any chance he's not my biological father?" I asked, hopeful.

"No. Your mother swears that she wasn't, well, with anyone other than him during the time before she found out she was pregnant."

I wasn't happy to hear this, but maybe Mom had not told Grandma the truth. I mean, I wouldn't have if I'd been faced with the same question. I might have done my best to tell the most convincing lie of my life. I'd seen pictures of Jeff Borden, and I didn't look like him, so maybe he wasn't really my father after all. I would have to ask my mother when she got home from her convention. She wasn't going to be happy I found out the truth, and she'd be mad at Grandma, too, for raising my curiosity. She knew how I could be sometimes when I was determined to find something out. She'd once told me I should be a detective when I grew up, but being a policeman didn't interest me at all.

If it turned out my mom's stepdad was my father because he raped her, I could handle it. I didn't know if my mom could handle it that I knew, but I guess we'd find out.

Before climbing into bed, I went online and searched for "children born from rape" and found out that most women who became pregnant get an abortion. Then I saw the really bad news. Apparently, I was the exception to the rule. It turns out that most children born from rape had a very hard time with life. Perhaps it was because I hadn't found out about it until I was thirteen, but most children born from rape suffered from depression and other mental illnesses. Maybe it was a good thing nobody ever told me. I wasn't sure, but now I knew, and I wondered how the news would affect my sanity.

Then I thought about all the children born that way, knowing their mothers might not have wanted them or were forced to have them the way my mother was. I also considered how crazy my grandma's ex-husband was to have forced my mom to give birth to me. I was happy she had, of course, but then if she hadn't, I wouldn't even know.

When my mom arrived home from her trip, I knew we would be having a very important talk. It was the kind of talk that would change everything about our relationship, and I had fretted about it for days. What if she told me she'd kept me only because she felt she had to? I couldn't imagine how that would make me feel, but I knew it wouldn't be good in any way.

I told Grandma I wanted to wait for at least a

day after Mom got home before bringing up what I'd found, but it turned out that didn't happen. We certainly never mentioned it on the phone calls she made while in San Diego.

Mom arrived home from her convention in San Diego that Tuesday afternoon about an hour after I got home. Her employee picked her up from the airport and when she got home, I didn't even go outside to greet her. This was suspicious, of course, but I was dreading the "talk" so much I wasn't exactly thrilled she was home, which in itself was suspicious.

Grandma had gone outside to greet her, urging me to do the same, but I refused. We had talked several times about talking to Mom, and she was well aware of my dread.

Mom entered the house and held out her arms for a hug. "Don't I get a hug after returning from being gone for several days?" she asked.

I went to her and hugged her. I realized I was the definition of mixed feelings. I was happy she was home but I had dreaded that moment as well.

"What's wrong? You feel okay?" she asked.

"Yeah. I'm fine." I stood there, doing my best to keep my composure, but that worked about as well as trying to stop a flood with a kitchen sponge. I burst into tears.

"What in the world?!" my mom said, pulling me back into her embrace. "What's the matter?" Then she said to Grandma, "Have you two been fighting the whole time?"

"No," Grandma said. "We've actually been getting along well."

Mom placed her hands on either side of my face and lifted it to look at her. "What's wrong?"

"I know!" I said, as if that would explain everything.

"You know what?"

Between sobs, I said, "About me! Where I came from!"

Her look told me she knew exactly what I meant. Turning an angry gaze on Grandma she said, "Did you tell her?!"

"No."

Looking back at me, she said, "Then how did you find out?"

I buried my face in her chest and sobbed, unable to speak. I wasn't sure if I couldn't say anything because of shame that I had snooped in her room or because I just didn't want to talk about it right then.

"Now that she knows, you have to deal with this," Grandma said.

"I know I do!" Mom said, her anger or frustration making her shout.

Then she held me close. "I'm sorry, baby. I didn't want you to know. None of it was your fault."

After I had stopped crying, we sat at the dining table and talked about things long held silent. I began to wonder how often people who love each other keep secrets that were this important. How many other details of my life—my existence—had been kept from me? What else did I not know? Part of me wanted to find out every detail that had been kept from me over the thirteen years of my life, but another part told me it was probably best that there were things I would never know. I began to realize that some secrets were better left kept that way. Would it have changed my life much if I'd never known I was born because my mother was raped by her stepfather? Probably not. But now I knew, and there would be no going back, even if I wished I could do that and never find my birth certificate.

Then again, it was a birth certificate. Something needed for such things as passports and other documents. Was it likely I would never have seen it? After all, one day my mother would die, and if I went through her things, including the locked box, I would have found it. Just how long did she think I'd not know?

"Shortly before I met the man I would marry, my stepfather raped me. I won't go into the details. For one thing, you're too young. For another, you don't really need to know them. From that one time, I became pregnant. I knew he was the father because I hadn't been with anyone else for nearly a year before that, and I wasn't with anyone else after that until I met your father, who adopted you once we were married."

"Grandma said he forced you to keep me and not get an abortion."

"Yes. My mother was unable to give him a child, and he wanted one, though he didn't want one so he could love the child but so he could claim himself a father. It was an ego thing."

"He sounds really weird."

"He was."

"You told me you always hated him."

"I did. Even more so after he did that to me."

"Did you want to abort me?"

She sighed deeply. "In all honesty, at first, I did. No woman wants the child of her rapist." She saw my look and rushed to reassure me. "But after you were born, I was glad I had you. I had considered putting you up for adoption, but I couldn't. What happened wasn't your fault, and I felt that giving you up would say it was. Besides, I wasn't a child anymore. It wasn't as if I couldn't take care of you. I was in my early twenties."

"I read that a lot of women get abortions when they're raped because they don't want a reminder of what happened. Is that wrong?"

"That's a personal choice. I chose to keep you after you were born. I didn't have the option of abortion because he refused to allow it. Other women would do differently. The world isn't a 'one size fits all' place."

"Couldn't you have snuck away to get one?"

Mom bowed her head for a moment before looking up. "Yes, I could have. I thought about it, even. But the truth is by the time I considered doing that, I didn't want the abortion anymore. I decided to bring you into the world and see what happened from there."

"Abortion's kind of a touchy subject for a lot of people," I said.

"Yes, it is. And it's up to each person to consider what they believe about it. It's not something someone can tell you what to believe."

We moved on from this topic to my life, specifically, how my mother felt about me. When she told me she loved me and always would, I accepted it.

Grandma came into the dining room where we were and asked if we were hungry. I wasn't, Mom probably wasn't much either based on how little she ate, but we said we were because we could see Grandma was.

That night, I considered that small act of saying we were hungry when we weren't. We were taking Grandma's feelings into account. I guess as much as anything, it's the small sacrifices and considerations that show we love each other.

The next morning, I woke up and felt a little bit different about myself, my mother, and my grandmother. In a weird way, this entire thing had caused us to grow closer. I was getting along with Grandma much better since I'd found out the truth about my past, and the destruction of the lie my family had lived made us stronger. I guess it could have gone the other way, but it didn't this time. Like Mom said, the world wasn't "one size fits all." Everybody's different. That's what makes the world an interesting place, I suppose.

When I arrived at school, I went to the cafeteria to meet my friends, but when I got there, bad news waited as if it had been biding its time until I handled one big problem before piling on another one.

Nick wasn't at school again, but it was the reason for that absence that became the problem. Tragedy had struck, and in a weird way, I was part of it. It's a wonder Nick forgave me for my part in it, but it took him a long time to do that.

Mia was at our table in the cafeteria, her head resting on her hands as she stared blankly at the tabletop.

"What's up?" I asked, not sure I wanted to hear the answer.

At first she said nothing, and I wondered if she'd heard me, so I repeated my question.

"I heard you the first time," she said.

"Then why didn't you answer?"

She looked up at me and I could see the tears brimming in her eyes. But I could see she was nearly done crying, not just getting started. She'd been crying for a while, based on the condition of her eyes and face.

"What is it?" I wondered if she'd found out that Nick's family had moved suddenly without a word, or if he'd broken up with her. That second one was inevitable over time, but I knew she would be devastated if he did that.

I sat beside her just as Cameron came up. Seeing the state Mia was in, she sat beside me, staring at the wreck that was now Mia.

"You didn't see the local TV news this morning?" Mia asked.

"No," Cameron said.

"What happened?" I asked. Okay, this couldn't be about a breakup, and it occurred to me it couldn't be about Nick's family moving away suddenly. Why would that be on the news?

"Nick's father is dead."

For a moment, I thought I would pass out. Dead? I suddenly prayed it was some kind of car accident or something, because what I was thinking

111

would be worse.

"How?" I demanded.

"Shot last night. Someone came to the door in the middle of the night and rang the bell. He went to answer it, and was shot. That's all they know right now."

"Did they catch the guy?" I asked.

"No."

"How do you know it's a guy?" Cameron asked. "Women shoot people too, you know."

When I said it just sounded like a guy thing to do, Cameron answered, "You're being sexist."

"Would you two stop arguing over something so stupid?!" Mia said. "Nick's father is dead! He must be devastated!"

I sat in silence, thinking about this. Nick's father must have been running from some people who were out to kill him. It was the only explanation. I wondered if the rest of Nick's family were in danger, including Nick. Those suspicious men had asked about him, after all. Was Nick in danger, too, or were they just wanting to find Nick's dad?

"Have you talked to Nick?" Cameron asked.

"No. I just saw it on the news. He doesn't have a cell, so I can't call," Mia said.

"I have to go to the bathroom," I said, giving myself an excuse to leave them for a moment.

When I got there, I entered a stall. I thought I was going to be sick, but after a moment, the nausea faded enough that I knew I wouldn't.

I suddenly felt like all the air in the world was settling on me, weighing me down. I sat on the toilet for several minutes, trying to get myself together. That's when the tears started. Soon, I was crying and unable to stop. A girl heard me and asked from the other side of the door, "Hey, you alright?"

"Yes," I said, though I wasn't sure if I was. My voice was all teary sounding.

When I had managed to stop crying, the first bell rang to send us to class. When we got there, an announcement came over the loud speaker telling everyone to come to the auditorium for a special assembly.

Several kids already knew about what had happened, but almost nobody really knew Nick at all since he was so new and hadn't made many friends. In fact, he'd made almost no friends at all other than Mia, Cameron, and me.

As we walked down to the auditorium, I heard one boy I didn't know say to a friend of his, "Jeez, it ain't my dad who was shot. Why do we have to do this, as if we knew the guy or his dad?"

I had run into this before, of course. There's this mentality in the world about how if it doesn't affect you, it's not important. People are basically a bunch of selfish pigs. I'd handled it before without saying anything, but this time it really set me off.

"A real nice guy's father was killed last night just because he opened his front door, you selfish pig!" I screamed at him.

"Calm down!" the guy said. "I just don't know why they're making us all gather in the auditorium like we were all his best friend." The guy moved away from me as though I was contagious.

A teacher came up to me and put her arm around my shoulders. Leaning in, she said, "Don't let it bother you. He's just being selfish, like you said."

I looked up and found Ms. Henderson, my English teacher, smiling at me. Her smile was sad and her eyes were red, as if she'd been crying. It made me feel good that an adult who didn't know Nick's father but knew Nick was sad about this, too.

"Thank you," I said. She had no idea how she restored a little faith in humanity for me. I also appreciated that she didn't haul me to the office for calling the boy a selfish pig, probably because she agreed with me.

When we were seated in the auditorium with our teachers, Mr. Lance, the principal, took the stage where a microphone had been set up.

Looking out at us for a moment, he turned on the mic and said, "I imagine some of you have already heard about the shooting last night of the father of one of our newest students. I'm sorry to say the man passed before medics could arrive. I want to make sure we all treat Nick Winslow well when he gets back to class. He'll need our support. Just imagine if someone you loved had been shot last night. I'm sure you'd want kindness and understanding when you got back to school. Treat Nick how you would want to be treated in that case.

"There are further developments that may or may not have anything to do with Mr. Winslow's death. A man who checked in at the Surfside Motel yesterday was found dead this morning from an apparent self-inflicted gunshot wound. Since shootings are rare in Denton, police are investigating the man to see if it's possible he killed Mr. Winslow before killing himself in his hotel room. I normally wouldn't tell you this, but I know you'll hear about it, and I don't want you to worry about your own safety. If the man who committed this heinous act is dead, he's no longer a danger to anyone. And if this isn't the man who killed Mr. Winslow, then the man who did is probably miles away by now. So again, rumors can fly about such things, but you're safe, regardless."

He talked a little more, but mostly I didn't feel any better. I had never considered that I was in danger, but I did worry about Nick. I desperately wanted to talk to him, hoping to measure how much to worry by his tone, but that was next to impossible. He had a home phone, but I didn't even know the number. The only way I could communicate with him was email, but I couldn't do that until I got home.

When I got home, I went to my room and lay on my bed and had the second cry that day. Then I went to the computer and opened my email and began to type.

I heard! I can't believe it! Are you okay? What about your mom and brother? What are you all going to do now? Are you moving again?? I guess it's obvious someone was after your dad. I am SOOOOO SORRY!!!!!! WB when you can!!!!

Loads of HUGS!!!!!!!!!!!!!!!

Maureen

As the afternoon crept into evening, I still hadn't heard back from Nick. I imagine he had other things to do, like grieve for his father. I understood, but it didn't make not hearing from him any easier.

When I did hear from him, I almost wished I hadn't.

14

Over the next few days, I made sure to watch the news on TV, something I had never done before. Mom heard about what happened, and she knew Nick was a friend. She held me and told me how sorry she was his father had been killed like that. That helped me feel better, but it scared me, too. What would I do if someone did something to my mom?

Grandma told me about a friend who died when they were in their late teens. She'd been killed in a car accident. She said another friend's mother died of cancer when she and the friend were only ten, so she knew how what happened made me feel.

I was grateful she felt this way, but it wasn't the same. Maybe the friend's death in the accident was, but neither of them knew the details about the death of Nick's father that I did. They didn't know about the constant moving or the men looking for Nick, probably to be able to locate Nick's dad and kill him, and they didn't know how I'd helped them.

On the news, they identified the man in the hotel as an FBI agent. He had been assigned to follow a man and now they were looking for the man he was following. They figured this guy had killed Nick's dad and then must have killed the agent after figuring out who he was, making it look like suicide.

I didn't have any more details than that, really, because the cops weren't saying much else. I figured they must have more information for them to come to that conclusion, though. I'd seen some interviews on the news of the guy in charge of the investigation, at least the guy from Denton. The FBI was part of the investigation now, of course, since the man in the hotel was an agent. The Denton detective on the case was named Robert Ebert. I hoped Detective Ebert or the FBI would solve the case. I wanted the man responsible for the murder to spend his life in prison at the very least.

I emailed Nick each day, and he finally answered. The email sounded as sad as he must have felt.

Maureen,

I think I might be responsible for my dad's death. I talked to this detective on the case and because I was alone, I told him about the emails to Ray and the one to me where he talked about those men. The detective didn't say it, but I could tell he thought they might have found us by hacking my friend's computer. I did some research and found out it's easy for someone who knows what they're doing to read someone else's email. I don't know what my dad did to make these people want to kill him. He was an accountant! My mom isn't talking about it, at least not to me or my brother, but I can tell she knows something about why we've been moving. She's probably told the cops what she knows. Anyway, I got my dad killed. My mom says we're going to move again soon but we can't yet because of the investigation. I think we're safe for now, though. A cop drives by about every hour or so. If it wasn't so dangerous and my dad hadn't been killed, I would think it was cool. It isn't though. They don't think anyone is after us, but they want to be safe about it. They say I can go back to school starting next week. I asked if I would have to have a cop with me at school, and they said I didn't. The detective said they wouldn't be after me since I wouldn't know anything. I'm not sure what they meant by that other than I didn't know why they killed my dad in the first place, so they wouldn't come after me. My mom, though. She knows. I can see it in her eyes just before she turns away and won't look at me when I look at her. I think she feels guilty too. I guess I'll see you Monday.

Nick

I read the email about ten times but I'd already started crying before the end of the second sentence. I just sat on my bed, reading what he'd written. After about the fifth time, I saw where he'd said at first that he "might" be responsible for his dad's death before saying later, "I got my dad killed." He must be feeling awful. I thought about how I'd feel if I felt responsible for my mom's death and just thinking about it made me feel sick and made my chest hurt.

Mom was working, and I thought Grandma wouldn't hear me crying, but she did. As I sat there, I heard a soft tapping on my door. Part of me didn't want her to come in and see me crying, but then I remembered how good it felt for Mom to hold me and tell me everything would be okay. Also, Grandma had dealt with death before, and I hadn't. She had said she understood.

"Come in," I said, my voice strained from crying.

The door opened, and Grandma came in. "Is it okay if I sit with you and we talk?" she asked.

I nodded to her and she sat on my bed next to me. For a moment, we just sat there, me crying and Grandma saying nothing. Then she put her arm around my shoulder and pulled me toward her.

I buried my face in her shoulder and sobbed for what felt like an hour. She just held me, saying nothing more than an occasional shushing sound. The shush wasn't harsh; it was more soothing. I could hear an "it will be alright" in the sound. I vaguely wondered if I would have heard that before when we weren't getting along. It occurred to me how sometimes people can misunderstand each other so easily. That always led to problems that wouldn't exist if they would just talk things out instead of believing what they'd thought they'd heard.

My sobs became quiet hitches of breath and finally stopped altogether. I just leaned into Grandma, aware of the wet spot on her top where my tears had soaked her.

"I'm sorry," I said.

"For what?"

"For soaking your top."

An arm patted my shoulder. "It'll dry."

I decided to come clean to Grandma and tell her about the emails. I explained how I had helped Nick create an email account and how that might have helped the men looking for Nick's dad to find him.

"Do you know if Nick told the police about

that?" she asked.

"He did," I said, grateful it wasn't now up to me to let them know.

"I'm so sorry this happened," Grandma said. Then she changed the subject. "Did Nick mention how he felt about all this in the email you got today?"

"He's sad," I said, wondering why she wouldn't see the obvious.

"Did he say anything that made you worry about him?"

This was a weird question. Why would I worry about Nick? I mean, other than he had just lost his dad and was upset by that.

"No."

"Good, then. Time will make everyone feel better about this."

I knew this was true even though being reminded rarely made anyone feel better.

We sat for a while until Grandma said, "Are you hungry?"

"No."

"Well, you have to eat something, at least."

"I don't want anything."

"I think a bowl of soup would be good for you. It's light and nourishing. And having a few crackers with it will help settle your stomach."

I wondered how she knew my stomach was bothering me then realized everyone's stomach gets upset when they cried like I had.

I knew she wouldn't take no for an answer so I said, "Okay." She hugged me against her before standing.

"Clean yourself up and come down in ten minutes. I'll have some lunch ready."

"Clean myself up?"

"Yes, dear. Your face could use washing and your hair needs to be brushed."

After she left, I went to my mirror and looked. She was right. My face was tear-streaked and my eyes were red. My hair looked like someone had taken a vacuum cleaner hose to it. I would have laughed at the sight if I hadn't been so upset.

15

Nick finally showed up at school about a week after his father's death. I saw him and my face lit up until I came closer and saw how upset he still was. He was just sitting at the table, staring off as if he was so deep in thought that he didn't notice anyone else around.

I sat across from him and tried my best to smile and talk to him, which was hard at first since he wasn't saying much at all. I was worried about him and I was also wondering if they were going to stay in Denton.

Finally, he spoke more than a few words in response to my attempts.

"My mom asked if I wanted to move back to California, but I'm still not sure. She said we could live there or somewhere else. She said she was looking forward to working again. She couldn't before because that would make it too easy to find us, I guess. My dad apparently had told her it might be easier to stay hidden if she didn't work." He paused before looking down and saying, "He didn't count on his son emailing a friend in California."

"You don't know that's how they found you," I said. "You have to stop thinking like that."

"My mom told me we had to move from Grand Rapids because my dad called his brother. He realized the next day that they might be monitoring stuff like that. You know, tapping the phones of our relatives. If they could do that, they could hack my friend's email."

"What did your dad do that was so dangerous to these people?"

"I don't know, but whatever they're hiding, it must be bad. The people who killed my dad weren't going away and forgetting about it."

"Does your mom know?"

"No. I asked her, and she said he wouldn't tell her anything for her own safety."

"But these people don't know that," I said and was instantly sorry I did.

He looked at me and said, "You don't think I've thought about that?" Then it hit me. He was as scared as he was sad, maybe more.

"My dad didn't even have a chance to get a shot off," he added.

"Your dad had a gun when he answered the door?"

He looked almost angry. "Of course he did! It was the middle of the night. He must have known it was someone sent to kill him."

That made me stop and think. Of course, he would have a gun with him. I might want one if I went to find out who was knocking on our front door in the middle of the night, and I'm not running from someone intent on finding and killing me. Then a thought struck me.

"But the guy didn't come in and kill you and your family. That must mean you're safe."

He just shrugged. "I don't know anymore. He killed my dad, and that's enough."

Mia arrived at the table and sat beside Nick, reaching out and pulling him toward her in a hug and even kissing him briefly. I noticed Mr. Lance looking at them but he didn't do or say anything. Public displays of affection, or PDA's, were forbidden, and teachers and administrators were always separating couples in the hallways. It never really stopped anyone from small kisses and stuff, but that also didn't keep the adults from telling us to stop. I figured he must have decided to let it pass since it was Mia trying to console Nick. I figured it would probably take dueling tongues for him to interrupt.

I still wanted to find out if Nick's mom was planning to move somewhere, so I did the interrupting.

"Nick, do you think your mom is going to move you back to California?"

This got Mia's attention. Her head jerked around and she glared at me. "Who said anything about moving to California?" She looked like my saying that might put things in motion for them to move, as if I was giving his mom the idea or something.

"It's a good question," I said.

"I don't know if she's going to do that or not," Nick said. "She kind of likes it here."

"There!" Mia said, still glaring at me. "Nobody's moving anywhere."

Cameron arrived, and I figured it was time to give Mia and Nick some time alone, or at least time without Cameron or me around.

"Let's go, Cameron," I said before she had a chance to sit down or even drop her bookbag. "I

125

need to talk to you in private."

Mia looked like she didn't care if we were going to talk about her and Nick. She just seemed happy we were going to leave them alone.

Nick seemed to flash me a look of apology, but I wasn't sure if I was right or not. It may have been a look that said he'd see me later. Or maybe it was a good riddance look.

I walked off and heard Mia say to Cameron, "You heard her. Go away."

"What's wrong with her?" Cameron asked when we were out of earshot.

"I asked Nick if they might be moving, and she freaked, like I was putting the plan in motion or something."

Cameron and I had talked about Nick's loss, and I had mentioned that I wasn't sure they would be staying in Denton. She agreed with me.

"I would imagine they would move back to Grand Rapids," she said.

I could have told her they came from California originally, but that would be breaking the trust Nick had placed in me. Besides, what good would that do? She would want all the details as to why he had moved so often, and I really didn't want to discuss that even if Nick wouldn't care. I felt enough guilt about my possible involvement in his father's death. I didn't want everyone else blaming me, too.

I expected Nick to be checked out of school that day, thinking his mom had decided they were leaving Denton that very day, so when the intercom buzzed during English and Ms. Henderson answered, the question the secretary asked surprised and scared me.

"Ms. Henderson?"

"Yes?"

"Do you have Maureen Lindstrom in class?"

"Yes."

"Could you send her to the office to check out?"

Me? Why was Mom checking me out of school? Had something happened? Was I being suspended for setting up an email for Nick that might have led to his father's murder? Had somebody we knew died?

Everyone in the room looked at me as if I was the luckiest person in the world to be going home from school early, but I didn't feel lucky. I felt doomed.

Gathering my things, I leaned over to Nick and whispered, "Will you be home later?"

"Yeah." To say it sounded like he didn't care if he was at home later or in an Egyptian desert would be an understatement. He had seemed like he didn't care about anything all day, and it worried me.

"What's your home phone number?"

He wrote it down on a piece of paper and handed it to me. "I'll call you."

"Whatever."

I left the room and did my best to hold back the tears, and this time I succeeded, at least for a little while.

Panic gripped my heart when I entered the office and saw that Mom wasn't the one checking me out. Grandma was.

When I saw her she gave me a little smile, but it wasn't a happy one. It was more like one of those,

"I wish I didn't have to tell you this" kind of smiles.

"What is it?" I asked, the panic spreading through me like wildfire through dried leaves.

Mr. Lance was standing there and said, "Maureen, could you and your grandmother step back to my office?"

I didn't want to go. I wanted to glue my feet to the floor. Bad news was waiting in his office. I could feel it the way I could feel the first chill wind of winter stream along my spine. This time I didn't try to stop the tears. I was about to get very bad news, and I wondered vaguely if I was being expelled instead of suspended.

"I don't want to!" I said through my sudden tears that had been waiting behind my eyes all day.

Grandma said, "Please, Maureen. We have to tell you something, and it would be better if you were not out here."

"What if I don't want you to tell me anything?!" I was being irrational and I knew it, but the sudden thought that Mom was dead grew from a quick worry to an absolute certainty. Why else would Grandma be here and not Mom? And how did she get here anyway? Mom drove the only car we had.

Grandma leaned down and said, "Shh, it's going to be okay. Everything is going to be fine. Just come into the principal's office with me."

I allowed myself to be led down the hallway to Mr. Lance's office. He closed the door and Grandma made me sit, though I felt more like running away.

Grandma sat beside me and said, "Your mother's been in an accident."

I knew it. She was dead. I felt my body want to collapse as I tried to get my breath. Suddenly, I felt unable to breathe.

"No!" It was all I could get out.

Grandma shushed me again and added, "She's at the hospital in Wharton right now, having emergency surgery. They told me it would be several hours, and I thought I would come get you so you could be there when she is brought to her room."

What? She was going to be alright? Did I hear her right?

"She's not dead?"

"No, dear. She's expected to live, but she has a long recovery ahead."

"What happened?" It was the first time I thought to ask that vital question.

"She had to drive into Wharton to get something she needed at the nursery. A drunk driver crossed into her lane and hit her car head on. The driver of the other car will survive, too, but he was driving rather fast when he hit her."

I didn't care about that. "She'll be okay?"

"Yes." It wasn't until then that I noticed the red in Grandma's eyes. She'd been crying herself earlier.

I burst into tears again, but these were tears of relief. I felt my muscles loosen from the tension they had been gripping.

"What was he doing drunk this early in the afternoon?" I asked, bewildered that someone would drink that much so early in the day.

"Some people are just like that," Grandma said,

pulling me to her and holding me.

"How did you get here?" I asked when we pulled apart.

"The highway patrol gave me a ride to the hospital, and I took a cab here to get you."

Mr. Lance spoke up. "I'll have someone drive you and your grandmother to the hospital in Wharton," he said. "That will save you cab fare back there, at least."

One of the secretaries seemed happy to drive us all the way to the hospital in Wharton. It was at least a forty-five minute drive with the traffic, and I was thankful she was doing this.

When we arrived, Grandma and I hurried to the surgery wing on the second floor. As we stepped up to the nurses' station, Grandma asked, "Is she out of surgery yet?" The nurse must have met Grandma already.

The nurse smiled as reassuringly as she could and said, "Not yet. If you'll sit in the waiting room, we'll let you know when she's in recovery." She pointed down the hallway to her right, indicating the waiting room was down there.

When we entered the room, another woman was there. She looked haggard, as if she'd been working twenty-four hours straight. She wore a pair of jeans that looked as worn out as she appeared, and a shirt that had threads fraying from the various seams. She looked like one of the homeless people who stood on street corners and begged money except that she'd obviously bathed recently.

She barely glanced our way when we came in and sat down, her elbow placed on the armrest of the chair she sat in, her head resting on that hand. She, too, was waiting for someone to either live or die as they endured surgery for whatever reason there was to be operated on.

I felt sorry for her. She looked as though she would be just as happy for a sudden heart attack to take her right now.

Finally, she turned her tired gaze on us. "You must be the lady's family," she said.

I wondered for a second how she knew about Mom. Then it hit me. This must be the wife of the guy who slammed into my mom's car. Or some relative of his anyway.

"Yes," Grandma said. "Are you related to the man who—" Grandma left the end of the sentence off, apparently not wanting to say the words.

"My husband. To be honest, I'm not sure how I want this to turn out."

I wondered for a moment what she meant by "this" until it hit me she meant his surgery. She'd be okay if he died? I was stunned. How bad would her life have to be for her to think this?

"Why does he drink and drive?" I asked.

I could see a dozen responses flit through her brain, but she must have discarded them in favor of a less severe answer. "It's just who he is."

She went back to resting her head on her hand, and I considered how bad her life must be. Did he hit her? A lot? Did he mess around with other women? Did he abandon her at times, disappearing for days or even weeks? My head teemed with questions that I knew would never be answered.

About an hour passed until a nurse showed up.

"Ms. Brickman? Your husband is out of surgery. They've taken him to recovery. He'll be transported to a room when he wakes up. If you'll follow me, I'll show you where that is."

When Ms. Brickman left, I asked Grandma, "I thought they couldn't operate on drunk people."

"They can. They just have to take some extra precautions."

About a half hour after Ms. Brickman left, the same nurse came to get Grandma and me. We were taken to a room and waited for them to bring Mom.

"When your mother gets here, don't react to how she looks. It's very likely her face will be bruised and stitched up. She won't look good, but believe me, she'll be fine eventually."

"I'm not sure I can do that."

"Just dig down deep and find the strength to react pleasantly. She won't want you to worry, and reacting badly will make her sad, and we don't want her to be sadder than she already is. When you see her, try to see her as she looked before the accident. Except for a few scars, that's how she will look again one day. She will need encouragement from both of us."

"I'll try," I said but wasn't sure I could do that. I'd never considered myself much for having inner strength, but maybe I could do it for Mom.

When they wheeled her in, half of her face was bandaged anyway, so we couldn't see any stitches. She had a black eye and bruises on the other side, but I did my best to ignore that, trying to smile at her instead. Because I was happy to see her alive, that wasn't as hard as I thought it might be.

Her right leg was in a cast running up to her hip. Her left arm was also in a cast, and I wondered what bandages and such covered her torso but put that thought out of my mind for the moment.

Be cheerful, I reminded myself.

"Hi, Mom!" I said, doing my best to hold back the tears that threatened to spill over anyway. I wanted to hug her but knew that wouldn't be a good idea. That could hurt, probably a lot.

She seemed to smile at me and reached out weakly with the arm that wasn't in a cast. I took her hand and held it until we left the room later, not letting it go for a second while remembering not to squeeze it too hard.

She said something that sounded like "hey."

"Don't try to talk," Grandma said, "unless you're in pain or really need something."

We sat there for about fifteen minutes, Grandma talking about how we would help her recover and me holding Mom's hand, doing my best to blink back the tears that threatened to start at any moment. I kept telling myself she was alive and it could have been much worse, though looking at her broken body kept reminding me it could have been much better, too.

Soon, the nurse who had brought us into the room came in and said Mom needed to rest now and that we could come back the next day during visiting hours, but only for a little while since Mom would need her rest.

As we left, Mom said, "Buh...of ooh." I knew what she meant: Bye. I love you.

We told her we loved her, too, then left.

We made it to the elevators before I burst into tears.

We took a cab to a car rental agency, and Grandma rented a car so we wouldn't have to pay for a cab everywhere we went. When we finally arrived home, it was nearing supper time, but I wasn't hungry. Grandma made some tuna fish salad and we munched on that with crackers.

We stayed up late, talking about how we would work together to help Mom recover, with Grandma reminding me of all that we would have to do until she was better. Mom took care of so many things around the house, including the grocery shopping, and all of that would now fall to us.

It wasn't until I was getting into bed that I remembered I had promised Nick I would call. Looking at the clock, I saw it was almost midnight, so calling now was out of the question. I would have to call tomorrow afternoon. I wouldn't be going to school the next day, so I wouldn't see him. Grandma said it would be fruitless for me to go since I wouldn't learn anything from lack of sleep and worrying about Mom. I was so busy worrying, I ended up forgetting to call Nick the next day as well.

As I finally drifted off, I said a prayer for Mom and Nick. It didn't even cross my mind to pray for myself. Their problems worried me more than my own.

16

Two days later, Nick lay in bed, staring at nothing. His alarm was about to go off to start another day, but he didn't feel much like starting anything. He wanted to lie in bed the rest of the day. No. It was more than that. He wanted to lie here forever and wait for the hopeless feelings to go away while knowing that wouldn't be long enough.

His mother, of course, wouldn't let him do that. To look at her, though, she seemed to feel the same way. His father's death meant more than a person now missing from the home. Its soul was gone now, too. A fourth of the family was gone, but he took ninety percent of its meaning with him.

Nick would hear his mother crying every night after he went to bed. He was sure his brother could hear her, too, since the sound of Jimmy's crying often mingled with their mother's in a sort of sad symphony.

The crying had ceased for Nick. He had heard of people describing how they felt numb from tragedy. He hadn't understood what they meant, but he did now. He'd give anything not to.

His mother tapped on his bedroom door and stuck a sleep-deprived face into the room.

"You need to get up," she said.

He heaved a sigh he didn't know was in him and said, "Okay."

She closed the door and moved down to Jimmy's room. Nick could hear the tap on Jimmy's door as if in the numbness his sense of hearing had tripled. He heard them exchange the exact conversation he'd just had.

That was another thing, he thought as he dragged himself from the bed. Their conversations had gone from lively to almost as dead as his father was. They rarely spoke to each other since the death except to say something required.

As he dressed, he remembered a conversation he'd had with Mia yesterday, if he could call it a conversation. She was still trying to convince him his life wasn't over without realizing most of his life had disappeared when his father died, probably because of him. She had tried hard to get him to talk to her, but he'd only given single-word responses or a shrug. She had finally angered him when she suggested he needed to just move on with life.

"You're alive. He isn't now. You have to pick up the pieces and move on."

He'd wanted to slap her but held back because his dad had always said hitting a girl was a coward's way of handling relationship problems. As he'd stared at her, all he could think was how her father was alive, her family was whole. She didn't have to know the numbness he hated, the near sureness that nothing meant anything anymore, and worst of all, the misery of being the probable cause of his father's death.

Instead of hitting her, he simply stood and left the cafeteria, which he felt was just another coward's way to handle the problem, but he knew he couldn't sit there and let her talk about what she was clueless about.

As he left his room to face another day he'd rather not face, he thought of how Maureen had said she would call, but she hadn't. He wondered what had happened. She was usually good at following through on things like that. If she came to school today, he would ask her what had happened to cause her to be checked out like that without warning. It had clearly frightened her, and the thought someone had died had gone through his mind like a sharp knife. He'd almost called her but felt maybe she wasn't calling because she didn't want to talk about whatever had happened. He could certainly understand that.

He went to the kitchen table to ignore his breakfast once again. His mom had toasted some Pop Tarts. She used to make bacon, eggs, and toast or biscuits at least twice a week, but she didn't seem to want to cook now, as if the death had killed that too. Or maybe she knew that taking the trouble to fix such a breakfast would only lead to throwing the food out, so why bother?

He managed to take a few bites of the Pop Tart because he knew she wouldn't let him get away with eating nothing at all, but it tasted like some sort of fruity sand mixture. He'd loved them before, but he no longer had a taste for anything.

Jimmy ate more of his Pop Tart than Nick did, but Nick could tell it wasn't exactly what Jimmy wanted either. They were both reduced to forcing themselves to eat out of necessity. The pleasure was now gone. Everything tasted…dead.

His mother gave them each their lunch money—no bagged lunches anymore either—and ushered them to the car. On the drive to school, Nick decided he had to ask the question that he and Maureen wanted answered.

"Mom?"

"Yes?" her response seemed tense, as if he might ask a question she wasn't prepared to answer, which he supposed his question would be.

"Are we staying here in Denton or moving back to California?"

He saw her glance at him in the rearview mirror, back at the road, and back at him before returning her gaze to the road ahead.

"I don't know. Do you want to move back?" She sounded almost afraid of the answer.

Nick considered it and realized his answer was completely honest. "I don't know."

Nick felt like an abandoned baby bird with nowhere to go.

They dropped Jimmy off at the elementary school before his mother drove the short distance to the middle school, where Nick was forced to face another day. *It is what it is*, he thought as he entered the school building that had started to resemble a dungeon.

17

The day I returned to school, I cried all the way there. I had wanted to stay home again, but Grandma said it would be better for me to have something to occupy my mind than to sit around the house moping the way I had the previous day after visiting Mom in the hospital. It also bothered me that Grandma didn't seem as upset as she should be. I mean, her daughter had nearly been killed in a car wreck. Grandma and I had started to get closer, but this opened up the ocean between us again. We rarely talked anymore, and when we did, it was about what we would do for Mom when she finally came home. I decided Grandma must not care, only pretending to love her family when she really detested all of us. And now, she was making me go sit through school as if nothing had happened. Fat chance!

I managed to stop crying by the time we arrived at school. I didn't want everyone to see me blubbering like a baby. Too many of the girls there hated me and would be all too willing to make my life even more miserable than it was by making fun of me. The taunts rolled through my mind as I walked into school, despite the fact nobody said anything to or about me until I arrived at the cafeteria and found Nick. Mia and Cameron weren't there yet, and it surprised me when he said, "Let's go somewhere else to wait for first bell."

"You don't want to wait for Mia and Cameron?"

"No."

I could see something was bothering him, and maybe he wanted to talk about whatever it was. I hoped it wasn't because I hadn't called him. Or maybe he was curious about what had happened to get me checked out early the day before yesterday. Still, we could talk about that around Mia and Cameron. I began to dread the coming conversation.

"Let's go to the arboretum," I said. Our school had this grassy area with a couple of trees there and a few benches for relaxing, as if we could just hop out of class to go chill outside. The school had named the small area the Sean Chaney Arboretum after a guy who donated a lot of money to various civic organizations.

As usual, we were the only people in the arboretum. Most kids avoided it because it was sort of out of the way and people could look at you through the large windows that surrounded the courtyard where the arboretum sat. Cameron had once said it made her feel like a fish in a fish bowl.

"What happened the other day?" Nick asked. He didn't need to explain his question.

Sudden tears returned, stinging my eyes like hot needles. "My mom."

Nick sat up as if expecting the worst news possible. "Huh?"

"She was in a car wreck. She's in the hospital."

"Aw, jeez. I'm sorry."

"Yeah."

We sat in silence for a moment. Suddenly, I felt kind of ashamed for being so upset about my mom. Nick's father had been murdered answering their door in the night. My mom was alive. At least people expected car accidents could happen. Getting shot dead when answering your door at night? That was light years from my tragedy.

"How are you holding up?" I asked, feeling he wanted to talk about it.

"You won't tell anyone?"

I braced myself for whatever he would say. A reply like that meant it wasn't good.

"No."

"I'm—well—I'm not doing so good."

I started to say *why not?* then caught myself. It was just one of those auto-responses people make. I was suddenly at a loss for words. Finally, I said, "I'm sorry." It was the absolute only thing I could think of to say, and it sounded as hollow to me as I'm sure it was to him, even though I was truly sorry. I decided to tell him how ashamed I felt for being as upset as I was about my mom. Maybe it would make him feel better to know that I could see my problem was nothing like his.

"Nick?"

"Yeah?" He looked like he wanted to run off and never speak to me again.

"I'm ashamed."

"Why?" I could see he really wanted to know, that it wasn't another auto-response.

"I'm all upset about my mom and it's nothing like what you're dealing with. She's hurt bad, but she'll live, and car accidents happen all the time.

It's sort of this thing we've gotten used to, like 'oh, well, another car wreck, what's for lunch?' you know? It's not like she opened the door to our house and someone killed her for no reason."

"It wasn't for no reason," he said. "I got him killed. Someone was after my dad, and my stupid email to my friend in California let that someone know where my dad was, and he came here and killed him." His face was twisting in a strange mixture of terror and rage. "He'd be alive if it weren't for me!"

"You don't know that!"

"Yes, I do! How else would they find out? He's dead because we opened an email account for me. And you helped! We thought we were so cool, fooling my parents, going behind their backs! But it got my dad KILLED!"

"You just think that! There's no proof you had anything to do with his death! Or me!"

"My mom told me we were running from these people my dad had worked for in California!" Nick shouted. "That he'd found something out that could be really bad for them, and that's why we kept moving like that!"

"What did he find out that was so dangerous?"

"I keep telling you I don't know! Stop asking me that! You think she'd tell me? Besides, she doesn't even know herself. She says he told her it was better if she didn't know!"

Again, it occurred to me that his mother's life was in danger now, too, or could be.

"Nick? Is your mother safe?"

"I don't know," he said, more quietly now.

"She says probably, but I'm not sure. She figures they would have known he wouldn't tell her anything to keep her safe, and like you said before, they didn't kill the whole family when they had the chance."

Stunned, I said, "But you're not completely sure, right?"

"Right."

"Your family's leaving town then?"

"We don't know yet. Mom isn't sure we are."

"But Nick—"

"Listen!" he said, cutting me off. "If something happens to my mom, I'm not sticking around."

"Where would you go? Do you have relatives somewhere you can move in with?"

"That's not what I meant."

"Then what did you mean?" The meaning of the answer I knew he would give, if not the exact words, hit me before he could say anything, and I felt as though a giant had come along and stomped me and wouldn't get off.

"I meant I'd go be with my mom and dad."

Silence filled the small open area. Not even the sound of the slight breeze reached me.

"You don't mean that."

"Yes, I do. If my mom dies, Jimmy and me will be orphans. We don't even have a grandmother the way you do. I've met the only grandparents I have, my dad's parents, only twice. They didn't even come to the funeral."

"Maybe your mom forgot to tell them," I said before realizing how stupid it sounded.

"I was there when she called them."

143

"Why wouldn't they come to their own son's funeral?"

"Who knows? I just know they weren't interested in coming and didn't even ask how Jimmy and I were. They don't care about us."

"How do you know that? Were you listening on an extension?"

"No. I was in the room. My mom told them my dad had been murdered. She listened a moment and said, 'I see,' and hung up the phone. All they'd said was, basically, they didn't care. They may have even hung up on her. She just put the phone down and cried.

"I'm sorry," I said. "But that doesn't mean you have to kill yourself if something else happens. Other kids deal with losses like this, and they survive it."

"Not me," he said. Then standing and hoisting his bookbag onto his shoulder, he strode off without looking back.

That day in our classes, he said nothing. Mia tried to get him to tell her where he'd been that morning, and he'd cussed at her and told her it wasn't any of her business. I could see that hurt Mia a lot. I know it would hurt me. Cameron took the whole thing in with both eyes and mouth wide open. We were all shocked at his words.

Of course, I knew where he'd been, but I wasn't sure I wanted to tell them. If I did, they'd want to know what we'd talked about, and I didn't want to tell anyone. It seemed too private. I mean, how often does your best friend say he might kill himself?

Looking back now, I suppose I should have said something. It might have stopped a lot of things from happening, but maybe it wouldn't have. With things like that, who can ever tell? It's like knowing whether Nick's email really was what led the killer to know where they were. It's an unknown. And sometimes what you don't know can kill you.

18

The next few days slogged by. Nick was barely talking, and Mia was coming apart over that, so I did my best to ignore them all.

I would go to school, come home, finish my homework, and eat something. Then Grandma and I would go visit Mom. In other words, I was miserable. I loved seeing my mom, but on the other hand, after we visited for a little while, I wanted to go home. We would sit there for an hour saying nothing. Grandma insisted on staying at least an hour, which usually turned into thirty minutes more.

The weekend came, and I wanted to do something else besides spend all day at the hospital, which Grandma had been hinting at. Again, I love my mom, but there are other things I needed to do. I wanted to visit her, just not for the entire day. I wouldn't want to spend all day with her if she was home and fine.

Visiting hours started at ten in the morning and went until three before resuming for the evening from six to eight. I could see us spending all seven hours there.

"You ready?" Grandma asked around 9:30 Saturday morning.

"Grandma, do we have to go for the whole time?"

"What do you mean?"

"I don't want to spend the entire visiting time there. We won't get home until 3:30."

"She's your mother."

She said this as if it was all the reason I needed to spend the bulk of my Saturday, not to mention Sunday, sitting in my mom's hospital room. It wasn't as if sitting there would make her heal faster.

"I know she's my mother!" I blurted louder than I intended. "But sitting next to her bed all day won't make her well again!"

"She appreciates the time we spend there."

"I'm sure she does, but I'm also sure she understands that I'd prefer not to stay there all day. I have a life, too!" I hoped she wouldn't challenge me on that and ask what I had to do that was so important because honestly, I didn't have anything to say on that. I just didn't want to spend all that time sitting and doing nothing in a hospital room, even if it was my mom's.

"How long do you want to stay?"

This was one of those trap questions where I had to find a middle ground. If I went too low, Grandma would be angry with me and argue, and if I went too high, I'd be stuck for that long, sitting and doing nothing while my mother mostly slept. Finally, I decided to just go for a round number.

"An hour."

"That's all?"

Dang. Too low.

"Your mom will hardly have time to say hello."

"She doesn't say hello anyway, Grandma! Not really. She just mumbles 'lo' and that's it. Then we're all silent until we're leaving. And even then, she just says 'buh' and we leave. It's not fair! If she could talk, I wouldn't be so against going for longer."

"She's getting better at talking," Grandma said.

"Maybe, but not enough to really carry on a conversation."

"It does her spirit good for us to visit."

"Fine, we can visit! Just not the whole time we're allowed to."

She stood glaring at me, her arms crossed, and I was reminded how our relationship was until very recently. I was feeling like she didn't really care for me again and she was seeing me as a burden. I didn't want that, so I said, "Fine. An hour-and-a-half?"

She huffed at me and said, "Okay. But I want you to talk to your mom about what's going on at school and how you're doing. She needs to hear those things."

I doubted she really needed to hear that, but I agreed just to make peace.

When we arrived at Mom's room, she wasn't there. The bed was empty and all made up as if waiting for the next patient. All the flowers she'd received and other stuff belonging to her were gone.

I stood staring at the empty bed, doing my best not to think the worst, which was impossible. I imagined a nurse walking in and saying, "Oh, we're sorry, but she died last night" as if it was nothing at all.

Grandma went to the nurses' station of the unit, which was called a step down unit. It was for people who weren't bad off enough for intensive care but worse off than those in a regular unit.

When Grandma came in, she was smiling and I could feel the tension wash off of me like dirt in a rainstorm. She didn't have one of those, "I'm going to make this sound as pleasant as possible" smiles. It was genuine. This would be good news.

"Your mother has been moved to a regular unit because she is doing so much better."

My knees felt wobbly, so I sat in a chair. For the first time, Grandma could see how worried it made me to find the room empty.

"Oh, honey. I'm sorry. I didn't realize you would think the worst."

I wanted to say I was her granddaughter, so of course I would, but I didn't.

After getting directions to her new room, we went there, but not before stopping at the nurses' station to thank them for the care they'd given my mom. Once we were on the elevator, she said, "Thanking people who help is always important, and nurses help more than most others. The doctors assign the care, but the nurses do the work. Without them, the world would be much worse off than it already is."

When we entered Mom's room, she smiled at us. "Hello."

I wanted to shout with joy! She wasn't mumbling anymore! Her voice was still kind of mumbly, but she could talk so much better.

"Hey!" I said, suddenly very happy we came to visit her today though I would never admit it to Grandma. I went to the bed and leaned over to hug her, and she hugged me back.

"I woke up this morning feeling so much better. The doctor said I could move out of the step down unit and get a standard room." She looked at Grandma. "How is everything at home?" I marveled at the fact she could speak in complete sentences.

Grandma filled her in while I sat holding her hand and smiling at her. For the first time, she was more like herself.

We ended up staying for two hours. Mom was the one who cut the visit short. "I know you don't want to sit around here all day, Maureen," she said. "Why don't y'all go home and you can see if a friend wants to spend the night or something. I'm sure life is lonely without me around."

I glanced at Grandma, an "I told you she would understand" clear in my expression.

We said our goodbyes and headed home. I called Cameron to see if she could spend the night. I would have called Mia, too, and made it a pajama party, but I knew all she would want to do is talk about Nick, and I wanted to avoid that topic.

Cameron asked her mom if she could stay at my place that night, and after getting permission, told me she could be over in about an hour. Her mom would drop her off.

That night was something I needed worse than I'd thought. Cameron and I talked, giggled, and squealed until Grandma came in to tell us to pipe down three times, getting more irritated with each visit. We finally granted her wish and whispered about everything we could think of until well after midnight. I know Grandma had gone to bed because the rest of the house was dark and quiet.

The next morning, we had breakfast. Later, we dropped Cameron off at her house before heading to Wharton to see my mom. I didn't argue about going this time. After all, it was much more enjoyable now that Mom could talk and was more herself.

Much later, I realized that part of what made me not want to go to the hospital to see Mom was that she was in such bad shape, and I didn't want to be reminded how bad off she was after the accident. Other things began happening, though, that sort of took over my life, and the next few months were even less fun than sitting silently in a hospital room wishing to be anywhere else.

The trouble started with Grandma and grew worse from there.

19

On Sunday, we learned that Mom would have to go into a rehab center for about six months. On the one hand, that was good news because it meant she was getting better, but on the other, it was bad because she wouldn't be home for another six months. Her employees could run the nursery business, so that wasn't a problem, but I would be stuck with Grandma and having to visit the hospital every day. While I loved seeing Mom, it was also a pain.

Monday, though, everything changed. Everything.

When my alarm went off, I showered and dressed before walking into the kitchen for breakfast. Grandma, an early riser, was not where she usually was each morning, sitting at the kitchen table and reading the news. I figured she was getting a late start and didn't worry, but as I ate, I wondered why she wasn't out yet. She had to take me to school when I finished eating.

When I had finished my cereal, she still hadn't come out of her room, so I went to look for her.

"Grandma?" I called as I went down the hall. Her bedroom door was closed, which only happened when she was asleep or getting dressed. That made me worry.

Tapping her door, I said, "Grandma?"

No answer.

"You alright?"

Still no answer.

I felt panic rise in me. Finally, I eased the door open. "Grandma?"

The first thing I saw was her unmade bed, which worried me more since she always made her bed as soon as she got up. Opening the door farther, I saw her. She was lying on the floor in front of her closet. She seemed to be struggling. Small groans and grunts were the only sounds she made. They were so soft I could barely hear her from just a few feet away.

"Grandma!" I yelled as I rushed in. Her phone was lying beside her. She must have tried to call 9-1-1. I snatched it up, but it was asleep, and I didn't know the code to open it. Rushing to the landline phone next to her bed, I dialed 9-1-1.

Seconds later, a woman said, "9-1-1, what's your emergency?"

"It's my grandma! She didn't come out of her room this morning and now she's lying on the floor!"

"Okay, take a few deep breaths. Is she conscious?"

"Well, sort of. She seems awake but she only groans and grunts." As I talked, I could hear the clicks of her typing into a computer.

"Are you at 391 Dover?

"Yes!"

"Okay, hold on, sweetie." I could hear her talking on another phone, giving someone our address. Then she was back with me. "Someone's on their way. What's your name?"

"Maureen."

"And how old are you, Maureen?"

"Thirteen." I wondered why she needed to know this about me. I wasn't the one who was lying on the floor barely conscious.

"Where do you go to school?"

Huh? "I'm sorry, but why would that matter?"

"It doesn't, honey. I'm just keeping you company until the medics arrive. Trying to keep you calm."

"Oh. I go to Denton Middle."

We continued chatting for a few more minutes until she said, "Okay, Maureen. The medics are pulling up in front of your house now. Could you let them in?"

"I can hang up now?"

"Yes, dear. You've been great."

"Bye," I said and hung up before rushing to the front door.

An ambulance with flashing lights sat in our driveway behind our rented car. A man and a woman were climbing out and hurried inside.

"She's in her bedroom!" I said as if they'd been here a dozen times before.

"Where is that?" the man asked.

"Down the hall. It's the last door on the right."

They hurried down the hallway, and I was right behind them as they knelt beside Grandma and began checking her.

"Have a seat on the bed," the woman said. Then she asked, "Can you tell me what was happening before this happened?"

154

I explained how I was eating breakfast and she hadn't come out of her bedroom yet. "I got worried and came looking for her. That's when I found her lying there."

"Is she your grandmother?"

"Yes."

"Where are your parents?" she asked.

"My dad's dead," I said. "My mom was in a car wreck last week. She's in the hospital."

Twenty minutes later, we were all in the ambulance, driving toward the hospital in Wharton, lights flashing and siren blaring. I was in the back with the woman and Grandma.

"What's wrong with her?" I asked

The woman looked at me gravely and said, "She's had a heart attack."

Sudden tears sprang to my eyes. "What? Will she be okay?"

"We don't know yet."

I prayed all the way to the hospital. It occurred to me that I'd heard that you don't really cherish what you have until you might lose it. I knew what that meant now.

Once we were rushed into the emergency department, they wheeled Grandma into the back, leaving me to sit in the waiting area.

"Can't I go back there with her?" I asked one of the nurses at the desk.

"We'll come get you as soon as we can. Just have a seat in the waiting area for now."

I sat down and suddenly realized there was nobody to stay with me at night. I thought about it and knew I couldn't stay with Cameron. She only had a small bed, too small for two girls our age. Her brother had his room, but if I slept there, where would her brother sleep? I wondered if they'd let me sleep on the sofa or something. Then I thought about their sofa. It wasn't that comfortable to sit on, much less sleep on. Where would I stay? Or if I stayed at my house, who would come stay with me? My only other relatives were my mom's brother and his family, and they lived in Germany.

I suddenly felt a need to talk to Mom. She was in this building, after all.

The nurse at the desk saw me approaching and said, "Not yet, dear. We'll let you know when you can go back."

"No, that's not it. My mom is here in the hospital, too. She's in room 528. Can I go visit her there?"

"Visiting hours don't start for another half hour," she said, looking at her watch. "You could go then."

I started crying, and the nurse said, "Oh, honey. Don't cry. Everything will be alright."

"You don't know that!"

"Okay, hold on a second. Let me call the unit your mother is on and see if they'll allow you to come up there."

She picked up her phone and tapped a few numbers. She spoke to the person who answered, explaining the situation and smiled as she hung up.

"They said you can come up and see your mom. Do you know the way?"

I looked around. "I've not gone there from here before, but if you can point the way to the front entrance, I can find it from there."

"You don't need to do that. It's much closer if you walk directly to her room from here." She turned and talked to a young woman probably in her twenties who worked there.

"Bridgette? Would you take this young lady up to room 528?"

"Sure," Bridgette said. Then she looked at me and said, "Come on." I liked her smile and smiled back.

On the way up, we chatted about various things, including why I was there in the first place and the dilemma I had realized I faced.

"Oh, dear. You mean you're all alone now?"

"Yes."

"You must be really strong to be able to handle all this. I'd be freaking out if this happened to me when I was your age."

I actually laughed a bit at this and said, "I am freaking out. I'm just good at hiding it."

Bridgette smiled at me and put an arm around my shoulders as we rode the elevator up to the fifth floor. She pulled me close to her side and held me there, comforting me.

"You'll be fine. I know a strong girl when I see one." I looked up at her and felt tension rush from me.

It's funny how we can meet people for only a few minutes that we may never see again, yet we never forget them. That was how I felt about Bridgette. I suddenly realized I would remember this moment fondly for the rest of my life, and that thought made me happy.

Bridgette escorted me to the nurses' station.

"I think Maxine called you about this one. Her grandmother has had a heart attack and is in the E.D. Her mom's the patient in 528."

"Yes," the nurse said. "You can go on in."

I thanked Bridgette and the nurse and went to Mom's room.

Opening the door, I peeked in. She was propped up and watching TV. Her breakfast tray was still on the little table that had been pushed out of the way to sit beside her bed.

Looking at me in surprise, she said, "Maureen, why aren't you in school?"

I burst into tears and rushed to her, leaning over and hugging her gently because I knew I could hurt her if I hugged too hard.

"What is it?" she asked, stroking my hair.

"Grandma! She's in the emergency room."

"Why?"

"She had a heart attack!"

"Will she be okay?"

"I don't know. They won't say."

Mom must have pressed the call button because the nurse I'd met at the desk came on the small speaker over the bed and said, "Yes?"

"Could someone come in here?"

A minute later, a nurse entered the room. "Yes, Ms. Lindstrom?"

"My daughter tells me my mother is here and she's had a heart attack. Could you find out what's going on with her?"

"Certainly," the nurse answered and left.

I sat with Mom, telling her about the morning's

events, until another nurse came in. "Ms. Lindstrom?"

"Yes?"

"It's true, your mother has had a heart attack. They've stabilized her and are preparing to admit her to the cardiology unit, but she won't be transported there for several more hours."

"Is she talking now?" Mom asked.

"I don't know. Once she's been admitted, I can escort your daughter to her room to see her, though."

We sat there for a minute after the nurse left and I remembered why I'd decided to come see Mom in the first place.

"Mom?"

"Yes?"

"Who's gonna stay with me?"

After a moment, she said, "I'll find someone."

We sat there for another two hours or so until the same nurse who'd come in last time walked through the door.

Looking at me, she said, "I can take you to see your grandmother now, but you can only stay in her room for a minute, just long enough to see her and, if she's talking, say hello. She needs her rest."

"Okay," I said, wishing Bridgette could take me there.

When I arrived at Grandma's room, she was asleep, so I didn't get to say anything to her. There was a nurse in her room when I got there, and I asked her if Grandma had said anything.

"She improved a bit and was able to talk soon after arriving," she said. "I know that because it's in her chart."

I breathed a small sigh of relief. At least she could talk. Reaching out, I patted her hand that lay on her stomach. "I love you, Grandma," I said. "Get well soon."

With that, I returned to my mom's room, having memorized the way. When I entered, she was on the phone. She sounded tired, and I was sorry this had happened to our family while she was laid up in the hospital. At least she was able to talk and do things now.

As I sat beside her, she said into the phone, "Thank you, Jenny. I can't thank you enough." They chatted for a moment more before Mom said, "Okay, she's back now. I need to tell her what's going on."

After she hung up, she turned to me. "That was Jenny Turner."

"Will I be staying with the Turners?" I'd met them before, of course. They were like my mom's second parents.

"Yes. You're going to stay with them until...well, until."

I knew what that meant. Either until Grandma came home or Mom did. Mom wouldn't be home for at least six months. Grandma? Who knew. The sudden thought she might die and never come home slammed me again, but this time I held it together.

"Jenny is going to come get you this afternoon and take you to the house. You'll need to pack a suitcase or two. She'll help."

I liked the Turners, but they were more like Grandma's age. He's in his sixties, and she's not much younger. I supposed it would be like staying with Grandma, but maybe a little more fun since they have a dog.

I mentioned that to Mom. "Do you think they'll let me play with their dog?"

"I'm sure they will. Be sure to ask Mr. Turner about his first dog. He loves to talk about him."

Around 3:30, Ms. Turner came into Mom's room and greeted her with a gentle hug while smiling at me.

"You're looking better than you did last week," Ms. Turner said. This was news. I thought Grandma and I were the only ones who visited Mom.

"Feeling better, too. I should be going into the rehab center in a day or two."

"That's great," Ms. Turner said. Then she looked back at me and said. "I suppose you're ready to get out of this place. Hospitals are no fun for anyone, especially girls who have a social life to maintain."

I smiled at her, silently thanking her for understanding what Grandma didn't. I wondered if I might have an actual good time staying with them. As I said, I'd met them plenty of times, but I'd never taken the time to get to know them. I mean, what girl my age really wants to get to know an older couple her mother is friends with?

I said goodbye to Mom and we left. As we walked to the elevator, Ms. Turner said, "Do you want to see your grandmother before we go?"

I considered it and decided against it. She would probably be sleeping, and they wouldn't want me to stay more than a minute anyway. "No, that's fine."

She put her hand on my shoulder blade and said, "Okay. Maybe we could stop and pick up a get-well card for her. Maybe get one for your mom, too. Would you like that?"

"Sure," I said.

Soon, I was in her car and we were driving back to Denton. I tried to relax, thinking the upheaval in my life was settling down now.

But I was wrong.

20

After I packed two suitcases with clothes and other things I would need, Mrs. Turner drove to where she and her husband, Jack, lived. He was an attorney, and she was a clinical psychologist, and they lived in one of the nicest homes in Denton. My mom told me that it was once the nicest home in town, but a lot of millionaires had moved there in recent years and built mansions farther inland. The house sat on a spit of land that protruded a bit into the natural harbor formed by Sugar Isle, which protected the shoreline from excessive wind and tides.

We carried the suitcases inside, and Mrs. Turner and I sat at a table in a tiny room overlooking the water, drinking a Coke. I suddenly remembered my manners and blushed that I hadn't thanked her for taking me in on such short notice.

"Oh, I forgot. Thank you for letting me stay with you and Mr. Turner. It's really nice of y'all."

"Don't mention it. I was so sure Jack wouldn't mind that I accepted your mother's request even before talking to him."

"He doesn't know I'm here?" I felt panic rising. What if he said he didn't want me there?

She chuckled. "He does now. I called him after talking to your mom on the phone. Don't worry. He's fine with it."

I relaxed a bit but still dreaded when Mr. Turner walked in. He might have just said okay to make his wife happy. He was a nice guy and all, but this was a big favor to do even for a close relative, and I basically barely knew them.

"Are you sure he wasn't just going along with it for you?"

"No, he doesn't do that. Believe me, he's thrilled you're here. We always considered your mom like one of our own children."

"Do you guys have any kids?"

She blushed before answering, and I thought maybe I had gone somewhere I shouldn't have. "No. I can't have children."

It was my turn to blush. "Oh, I'm sorry I asked."

"No, dear. Don't worry about that. It would be one thing if you knew and were trying to cause me grief, but you were just asking a question. Life is what it is. Yes, I wanted children, but rather than have my own, I get to be a sometimes mom to others."

"How?"

Smiling, she said, "Well, first there's you right now. From what I understand, you'll be here for several weeks at least, possibly months, depending on your grandmother's recovery. I'm too old to be your mom, of course, but not too young to be your grandmother. And second, there was Bridge Over Troubled Water, a group Jack and I started."

"Oh, yeah, my mom mentioned that. She said that's where she met you and Mr. Turner. It's a place where kids went to talk about their problems."

"Yes, and please, call us Jenny and Jack. We don't like being called Mr. or Ms., or even Mrs. by people we think of as friends. It makes us feel old, and though maybe I am old, I don't have to sound like I am."

"How old are you?" I asked, then quickly added, "you don't look old at all."

She chuckled again. Her laughs weren't insulting. They showed she was amused by me more than anything. I appreciated them. She liked me and my company.

"Don't be embarrassed. Just keep it between us girls. I'm fifty-seven." She smiled at me again, that same warm, friendly smile.

I smiled back at her, beginning a new chapter of our previously unimportant relationship. I liked her, and she liked me. I felt welcome and relaxed.

Then I remembered something important. "The car!"

"What about it?"

"My grandma rented a car after my mom's accident. It's still in the driveway. She's getting charged for it every day."

"Don't worry. I'll get the key and return it to the rental agency tomorrow."

I relaxed. I could picture Grandma having to pay thousands of dollars for a car that had sat in the driveway for weeks.

"Where's your dog?" I asked, now that the problem with the car was settled.

"Bluebelle? She's out back. You want to go see her?"

"Sure!"

We went outside, and I played with their dog, Bluebelle. She was some kind of hound like you'd see with a bird hunter, and she had one blue eye and one brown.

"Is she blind in the blue eye?" I asked as I threw a ball for her to run after.

"No. That's a common misconception. It's just a genetic anomaly."

Bluebelle ran back to me with the ball and circled me a few times before coming to stand in front of me, where she dropped the ball and grinned, begging me to throw it again. I did, and she bounded across the yard, snatched it from the ground as she ran past it, and repeated her loop and stopped back in front of me, the slobbery ball lying at my feet. She again panted and smiled at me, obviously happy someone new was there to throw her the ball.

After tossing the ball a few times and ending by petting Bluebelle, who rolled onto her back for a good belly rub, we went back inside.

"Want another Coke?" Jenny asked. I didn't tell her Mom only allowed me one per day, figuring if it was important to Mom that the rule remain in effect, she could tell Jenny.

"Sure," I said, hoping she didn't detect my surprise at the offer.

As we sat again, I said, "Mom told me to ask Mr. Tur—I mean Jack—about his first dog."

"Bones, yes. He did love that dog."

"What was he like?"

"I never knew him. Jack got him when he was about your age. We've had dogs since, and we love them dearly, but Bones will always hold a special place in Jack's heart."

"Because he was his first?"

"Maybe, but mostly because—well, I'll let Jack tell you."

We went on to other topics, including whether or not I had a boyfriend.

"I have a friend who's a boy, but he's not really my boyfriend. He's just my best friend."

"Oh? Who is he?" I could tell from her look that she thought maybe I was playing down the whole boyfriend aspect to our friendship.

"No, really. He's just a good friend. His name's Nick. Nick Winslow."

She stared at me for a moment in a sort of mild shock. "You mean the son of the man who was murdered when he opened his door to someone in the night?"

"Yes."

"That was terrible," Jenny said. "I felt so bad for the man's family."

I wondered if I should say something about how Nick blamed himself but didn't.

"Yeah, Nick's pretty torn up about it."

"I would imagine so," Jenny said.

We changed the subject again, this time to school and whether I liked it or not. Time went by quickly, and we ended up laughing a lot.

When Mr. Turner—or Jack—arrived home that evening, Jenny went to the kitchen to fix dinner, which would be homemade pizza to celebrate my arrival to become a temporary daughter to them— her words, not mine. Jack and I sat at the same table

Jenny and I had when I arrived.

"I'm sorry about what happened to your grandmother and mom. They're both lovely ladies."

Okay, Mom could be lovely, but it wasn't a word I would use to describe my grandmother, despite how we'd grown closer since she moved in.

I wasn't sure how to respond, so I just thanked him.

"I bet you're nervous, wondering what will happen to your grandmother, how long you'll have to stay with us two old folks you barely know, and if Jenny is good at making homemade pizza. You know, important things like that."

I smiled at his attempt at humor. It wasn't that funny, but I saw it for what it was—an attempt to make me feel better—and appreciated it.

"I'm hoping I don't get in the way. I can do that sometimes."

"Nonsense. By the time you move back home, we'll all be secretly wishing you could stay here."

The pizza was great, the best I'd ever eaten, and I told Jenny so. She thanked me. After dinner, I asked Jack—I was getting used to calling them by their first names by then—about Bones.

He smiled, sighed, and said, "You mean the greatest dog who ever lived?"

"I guess."

"Are you sure you want to hear this? Jenny says once I'm on that topic, it's hard to get me off of it."

"Yes. I love dogs. I want one, but Mom isn't sure yet."

He went on to tell me about his first dog and

how he came to be named Bones in the first place. The story made me sad and happy at the same time. I couldn't imagine anyone letting a dog starve the way Bones's owner before Jack did.

He told me about how Bones saved the lives of his friends and him when they went camping one time in an area that was now a neighborhood in Denton, and how he had to carry Bones several miles to the vet's to get stitched up from being attacked by a Florida cougar that had come along where they had been camping.

He explained how finding Bones led him to meet the man who ended up raising him, more or less, and how he'd met a woman named Mrs. Dawson that he'd worked for as a gardener and how later my mom held that same exact job.

"Mom talks about Mrs. Dawson a lot," I said. "She says she was a great woman."

"That she was," Jack agreed. "She even took your mom in to stay when she had a fight with your grandmother and moved out. Your mom had a difficult life as a teen."

"I know. She told me," I said. Then I changed the subject to keep from talking about that.

"Have you had other dogs besides Bluebelle?"

And so it went. We talked until my bedtime, after it really, and by the time I went to bed, I felt like I belonged there.

I would try to rekindle my friendship with Nick the next day. Jack and Jenny wanted to meet him.

21

We received a call from Mom that night telling us that Grandma was better and awake. She'd spoken to her on the phone, and she had mostly been concerned with all the fuss she'd created. Because she was better, I wasn't as worried. It had been a fuss, but at least now things were better.

When I went downstairs to breakfast the next morning, Jenny and Jack were having theirs already.

"We're early risers," Jack said. "Having a dog that needs to go out can cause that."

Bluebelle bounded up to me, and I rubbed her behind the ears as she smiled up at me. It was almost as if she was telling me how happy she was I hadn't gone home.

Jenny said my plate was in the oven keeping my food warm. She had made scrambled eggs, bacon, and grits with butter.

"The bread's in the breadbox, and the toaster is on the counter, and there's orange juice and apple juice in the fridge. Help yourself. We'll need to leave in about a half hour to get you to school on time," she said.

I was happy she didn't get up and do for me. I understood about the cooked food, but I could do the other stuff for myself. If they fussed over me like I was a guest, I would have felt bad.

I finished breakfast and we loaded into Jenny's car. I would be getting the assignments I missed yesterday and wasn't looking forward to my day because of that. I knew I would have extra homework tonight.

Jenny brought me to school later than Grandma did, so Mia and Cameron had arrived, but it turned out Nick wasn't there, and his absence made me nervous. He'd not said anything else about taking his own life, but I knew he was still thinking about it, mostly because he sort of moped through life now as if nothing mattered. He didn't do his homework anymore, and his grades were suffering. I'd seen a test from math class we got back, and he'd failed it. I wasn't a math whiz or anything, but I paid attention in class enough that I passed it with a 90.

After dropping my absence excuse and another note about taking a bus after school at the office, I went to the cafeteria to meet my friends.

"Is Nick not here?" I asked in case he'd gone to the bathroom before I arrived.

"No," Mia said. "But even when he's here, he's not, you know?"

Yeah, I knew.

"What's with him? I mean, I know his dad was killed, but life goes on," Mia continued. "He needs to snap out of it."

"It's not that easy," Cameron said.

"Where were you yesterday?" Mia asked. She'd avoided Cameron's comment, and I knew Mia well enough to know it was because it didn't fit her views. Her question sounded like she was accusing me of skipping school or something.

"My grandma had a heart attack," I said.

Both their faces showed the shock that response triggered. I'd purposely made it sound like I was saying I just didn't feel like coming to school to play it down.

"Oh, my God!" Mia said. "Is she okay?"

Cameron fielded that one. "Jeez, Mia! She had a heart attack! It wasn't like she caught a cold!"

"I meant is she going to be okay! I know a heart attack is serious!"

"She's doing okay, I guess," I said. "She's in the hospital for a little while."

"Your mom and your grandma were in the hospital last night? Did you stay at home alone or something?" Mia asked.

"No." I so wanted this conversation to end.

"Then where?" Cameron said. "You coulda stayed at my house."

I explained to her why I couldn't, as I'd realized in the hospital. "I stayed with the Turners."

"You mean the attorney and his wife? The ones your mom knows real well?" Cameron asked.

"Yeah. They're nice, and they have a dog." I went on to explain about Bluebelle and how much fun I had with her.

"Cool," Mia said.

We continued chatting until the bell to go to first period. I had a quiz to make up and was sent to the library to do that. My teacher had loaded the quiz into the school's computer system and given me the password to load the quiz, and I left class for the library.

After finishing the quiz, I went back to class, thinking about Nick and praying he would be alright. I didn't know if I could handle it if he did something to himself.

That day was a tough one for me. Besides worrying about Nick, I was also worried about my grandmother, not to mention my mom. It felt like everyone I cared about was either hurt, sick, or seriously depressed. At lunch, I realized that wasn't exactly true. I was beginning to care a lot about Jack and Jenny, and they were fine.

For now, the evil voice in my head told me, the one that tried to convince me that no matter what I did, bad things were all that lay ahead for me. By the time I left school, I really was feeling like my life was jinxed, and that anyone close to me was going to suffer just because they were people I cared about. Even my grandmother's heart attack had waited until after we had more or less started to get along and start forming a bond.

I'd been told to take a school bus to Jack's office that first day. He owned a building that had a number of offices inside, including a real estate office and an insurance office. I climbed down from the bus and walked into the building.

I was shocked to see that Bridgette was the receptionist for Jack's office.

"Bridgette?" I think my mouth hung open. How could she work at the hospital in Wharton and work here, too?

She looked at me and laughed. "No, I'm Brianna. Bridgette's my twin sister. Did you meet her in the emergency room at the hospital once?"

"Oh, that explains it. Yes, I met her yesterday."

"Are you the girl she walked to your mom's room?"

"You know about me?"

"Yes, she talked about this sweet, pretty girl she escorted to her mom's room."

"Wow!" I couldn't believe Bridgette had actually talked about me to her sister. "You two look exactly alike!" I said, marveling at that fact.

"That's because we're identical twins. We used to play a lot of tricks on people with that."

"I bet you could do that!" I said. "I bet your mom couldn't even tell y'all apart."

"Actually, she and our dad are the only ones who can. We've never been able to fool them." That amazed me as well. I didn't think I would ever be able to distinguish one from the other. If I lived in the same house with them, I'd need to put a tattoo on their foreheads or something to tell them apart.

Finally, she turned the conversation to the situation at hand. "So, what can I help you with? I'm pretty sure you don't need a criminal attorney."

"No," I said, laughing for the first time that day. "I'm staying with Mr. Turner and his wife while my mom and grandmother get better in the hospital." I used his last name because I didn't want to seem impolite.

"Oh, Jack mentioned you, too! I had no idea you were the same person my sister met yesterday!"

I was a little shocked that I seemed to be the focus of several conversations between someone I had met and someone I hadn't. Maybe shocked isn't the right word. Awed? Flattered? I don't know, but it felt weird and awesome at the same time, especially since Bridgette had been one of the people who'd talked about me when I wasn't there or anything to spur a conversation.

And she said I was sweet and pretty! I had really liked her, and now I was talking to her identical twin. As my mom liked to say, it's a small world. Just meeting Brianna was making my day much better.

"Let me let Jack know you're here," she said and picked up her desk phone. She punched a few numbers and said, "Jaz, could you let Jack know that—" She looked at me. "Oh, dear, I didn't catch your name."

"Maureen."

She turned back to the phone and said, "…that Maureen is here?" She listened and said, "Okay." Brianna said, "You're expected. Go on back."

I looked around. This was the first time I'd been in this office and didn't know which was his. "Which door?" I asked.

"Oh, sorry, hon." She pointed at a door that had a small sign that read, "Mr. Turner." I'd not seen that detail before.

"Thanks," I said. "And tell Bridgette I said hello."

"I certainly will. She'll be so surprised that I met you." She smiled and waved at me as if I were the most important person she'd ever met, which made me feel really good, and I walked through the door to Jack's inner office area.

A woman smiled at me and said, "Hi, Maureen.

I'm Jaz, short for Jasmine. I'm Jack's secretary." She pointed at a chair nearby. "You can have a seat there. Jack will be with you in a little while. He's with a client, so just make yourself at home."

I sat in the thickly padded chair and felt my body sink into the fabric. It was the most comfortable chair I'd ever sat in.

I considered how nice people could be while I waited. I'd barely met Bridgette, yet she had actually talked about me with her sister. Then Brianna had been so nice to me as well, even though she really didn't know me at all—just as Bridgette hadn't. People were mostly nice if you give them the chance.

As I sat there getting sleepy in the most comfortable chair in the world, an older man walked through the door and spoke to Jaz. He had lots of tattoos on his arms and even a few on his face. They looked old, like him, as if they'd been put there many years ago. I noticed Jaz point towards me and speak, and the man turned to face me.

If I hadn't been in Jack's office with someone who obviously knew this man, I would have been a little scared. He looked like the kind of man I would be expected to avoid, with his many tattoos and scruffy appearance.

He stepped toward me and held out his hand.

"Hi, Maureen. I'm Tom. I'm Jack's chief investigator."

"You mean like a cop?" I asked, shaking his hand.

"Well, not exactly. I just investigate things and

people that Jack needs information about. That sort of thing."

"I was wondering why you didn't have a gun if you were a cop."

He chuckled. "To be honest, I'm an ex-con, so I can't legally carry a gun. I'm not even allowed to get a license as a private investigator, but Jack uses me anyway."

My look must have told him my reaction to this news. "Don't worry, though. I'm harmless now. Jack changed who I am."

"Really?"

"Yep. He's the best person I ever met."

Jaz, who'd been on the phone, hung up and said, "You can go in now, Tom."

Tom gave me a little salute and winked at me. "You take care, little lady," he said and walked through the door that I assumed went into Jack's office.

"Is he really a nice guy?" I asked Jaz.

She smiled. "The best. Don't let his appearance fool you. I'd trust him with my life."

She turned back to her work, and I settled back into the chair. As I sat there, I could feel sleep sneaking up on me, but for some reason, I didn't take steps to stop it.

In what seemed like seconds, I was being shaken awake. I startled and found myself looking into Jack's smiling face. Tom was standing behind him, grinning.

"Comfortable chair, isn't it?" Jack asked.

I blushed, mortified that I had fallen asleep like that in his office. "Yeah," was all I could muster.

"Tom tells me the two of you have met. He's going to take you home and sit with you there until Jenny gets home. You can even take Bluebelle with you and y'all can play in the yard if you want. Just don't let her tucker you out throwing her ball. You seem pretty tired." I looked down and saw Bluebelle sitting quietly beside Jack's leg.

"No, I'm okay," I said, trying to figure out the meaning of what Jack had said.

"Tom's taking me to your house?"

"Yes." He looked at Tom and then back at me with a smile. "Don't let his appearance fool you. He's maybe the nicest man I know. He and his wife have two daughters and a son."

"Are they my age?"

"Sorry, no. They're older," Tom said. "But they survived having me as a daddy."

I guess they could tell being with Tom made me nervous, but I also knew Jack would never allow someone dangerous to be alone with me.

Getting up, I stretched. "How long was I asleep?"

Jaz answered, "About twenty minutes, I guess. I don't think you lasted much longer after meeting Tom."

I felt the side of my face was wet, and I wiped it hurriedly with my hand. I blushed again because I had apparently drooled in my sleep.

"Don't let it bother you, kiddo," Tom said. "I've looked a lot worse after waking up, and I've fallen asleep in worse places. Come on. Let's get you and Bluebelle home."

Grabbing my bookbag, I followed Tom out,

and Bluebelle followed me. I found it strange that she was there. Where was she kept?

When I asked Tom that in the car, he said, "She stays with Jack most days, unless he has court scheduled."

"Really?"

"Yep, really. I sometimes wonder if he loves Jenny or whoever his current dog is more." He chuckled at that and drove me home.

On the way, I asked him what he had been in prison for.

"Drugs. I made a lot of mistakes in my life, starting with how I treated Jack when we first met."

"Oh? You weren't nice to him?"

"Not at all, but he eventually taught me the value of being a good person. He's the greatest man I've ever known."

Once I finished playing with Bluebelle and came back in for a Coke, Tom told me the story of how he treated Jack when they were kids. First, I was amazed they'd known each other that long ago—both men were in their sixties. Second, I realized how love changes people. That's most of what Tom talked about, how love changed him— love from Jack, Jenny, and his wife and kids.

When Jenny arrived home later, I said goodbye to Tom. I liked him, too. Yes, there truly are a lot of great people in the world. I felt more people would realize that if they'd stop judging people based on their appearance. Then I remembered I had judged Tom by his appearance at first and hoped I could stop doing that.

That night before bed, I decided to send Nick an email.

Hey, Nick!

I'm sorry I missed you yesterday. My grandma had a heart attack, but it looks like she'll be okay. I wanted to see you today because, you know, we're best friends.

I hoped that last sentence was still true. I thought some more about what I wanted to write. We'd not spoken much since that morning in the arboretum, at least not about the stuff that mattered, and I wanted to talk about it, just not in an email. Mostly, I wanted to let him know we needed to talk. I went on with my email.

Let me know that you got this email. I really want to talk to you about some things. Remember (PLEASE!!!!) that I am your friend. It's just that I'm worried about you and feel I need to talk to you about some things.

Love (though not like THAT),

Maureen

I pressed SEND and watched the email disappear from the screen, hoping he would get the message and would email me back.

22

Nick skipped school the following Monday. His mother had dropped him off, but instead of going into the building, he waited until his mom had driven off and walked around to the back, through the soccer field, and into the woods that lay beyond. His mother had recently taken a part-time job, and she would be headed there now. She said working at a place where she was constantly being kept busy helped her forget about his dad.

Nick, though, didn't want to forget. He thought it was terrible his mother did. He had started seeing her as some kind of betrayer, as if her desire to forget her husband, his father, was some kind of act of treason.

He hated her for it, and he hated himself for hating her.

He'd been told that he would feel better as time passed, but so far that hadn't happened. He still felt his father's loss each day, like a painful splinter that refused to be removed. Like a splinter, the ache was constant but would become sharper whenever something touched it. All anyone had to do was mention his father, and it was as if they'd squeezed where the splinter lay.

This was why he'd abandoned the girls who had become his friends. They wanted to talk about his dad and almost nothing else, as if they thought they could squeeze the splinter until it didn't hurt anymore.

He missed the times with them, the laughs and the attention they gave him, but once the attention turned painful, he couldn't handle it anymore. He'd said nothing to them, just stopped talking to them.

He'd expected to miss talking to Mia because she was about more than talking. However, he missed Maureen the most because she was almost all about talking, and now he had nobody to talk to. He could talk to his brother, Jimmy, but what good would that do as far as the pain he felt? Jimmy was going through the same pain.

Maureen had emailed him. He'd read the email, but he'd not replied. She would figure out that he didn't want to be in touch with her anymore. Their friendship had ceased to exist.

Then again, he'd probably no longer exist either. He'd felt his death approaching the way you could feel a storm approaching because of the distant thunder. Thunder seemed to be everywhere in his life, and he didn't know what he could do about it.

Other than die. That was something he'd not told any of his friends. He'd thought of killing himself many times, even before his father's death. Now, he saw no reason not to do it.

He walked the two miles home. When he entered, the house felt eerie, as if he'd chased away a few ghosts upon entering. He wondered if he would join them when he died. Mostly, he hoped to join his dad, and if he was a ghost living there now, that's where Nick would be, too.

Going to his room, he lay on the bed for a few minutes, wondering if there was something he could use in the house to kill himself. They owned no guns, and stabbing himself with a knife would be too bloody and very possibly not fatal. He thought it would be hard to stab himself anyway, especially knowing all the gore he'd leave for his mom to find if he was successful. He wanted to just go to sleep and never wake up. Then when his mom found him, he'd just be lying there, physically whole. That way he wouldn't haunt her dreams or memories as much.

Then he thought about sleeping pills. He'd seen on TV about people who killed themselves that way. He'd heard it sometimes happened totally by accident, so it couldn't take many pills to do that. Five, maybe? Six? He would just go to sleep and never wake up, as he wanted to do.

He also knew his mom sometimes took sleeping pills to help her sleep. It was something she did sometimes even before Nick's father died.

Rising from his bed, he started toward his mother's bedroom. Entering, he went into her bathroom and began rummaging through the drawers. Opening the second drawer, he noticed a number of prescription medicines, some of them expired. He wondered if taking an expired medicine would kill him but decided against it since it likely wouldn't do much more than make him throw up, if that.

Then he saw it. Ambien. These were his mom's sleeping pills. He read the instructions on the bottle. He noticed there was a warning sticker to say that taking too many could cause serious harm or death. It didn't say how many were too many, but he figured it wasn't much, based on what he'd seen on TV.

He noticed that each pill was only ten milligrams. He figured sixty milligrams would certainly be enough since one pill was the prescribed dosage.

His mouth was dry as he shook out six of the small pills, so he turned on the faucet and took a quick drink before taking the pills. Capping the bottle, he set it on the counter, popped the pills into his mouth, and leaned down to the running faucet, taking several gulps.

At first, his stomach wanted to rebel and vomit the pills and water up. He blamed this reaction on his nerves. It wasn't every day he decided to kill himself, though he'd been thinking of it for a while now.

Going back to his room, he lay on the bed and waited for sleep. He figured after that, his breathing and heart rate would slowly dwindle to nothing, and he'd be with his dad.

One of his last thoughts before drifting off was of his dad and the happy expression he would have upon seeing his son again. Then he thought about the suicide hotline, but it was too late for that now. The decision and resulting action had taken place.

"See you soon, Dad," Nick said to the mental image of his smiling father before drifting off.

23

When Holly Winslow left work just after two o'clock, she drove straight home, where she hoped to take a nap before the boys arrived home around 3:45. She took them to school each day, but they rode the school bus home to allow her time in the afternoon for shopping and other necessities of life. Sometimes, one of those necessities was more sleep. She'd not slept enough since Brad's death, and because there was little else that needed doing that afternoon, she hoped to indulge herself in trying to catch up.

She had not made up her mind yet whether they would move again. She was tired of moving, and it appeared she could be found whether she ran or not. Brad hadn't told her the details of why they ran in the first place, other than to tell her he'd found evidence of a huge crime where he worked—a crime that could have dangerous results for him if he remained in California.

Their first move was to Michigan, of all places. Brad had hypothesized that since he'd lived his entire life in warm climates, they probably wouldn't look for him in a snowy place like that.

But several days after he had called his brother to talk about the disappearance, but not their location, he had seen a stranger looking at him one day in a grocery store, seeming to check him out and even follow him. He'd panicked, and they'd moved immediately to Florida, figuring that if they could track him to Grand Rapids, they might as well live somewhere warm.

She'd tried to convince him that he was being paranoid about the stranger, but he'd insisted, finally saying, "Holly, this is life or death for me. I don't have the luxury of dismissing even a slight possibility that they've found me."

When she'd pressed him for details of the crime he'd found, he'd refused, telling her he didn't want to endanger her life as well. She asked how they knew he'd found out whatever it was, he'd confessed that he had asked his boss about it. "Stupidest thing I've ever done," he'd said.

Now, she was required to work to help make ends meet. She would have to find a full-time job eventually, but she felt she could handle only a part-time one now, working from 8:30 to 2:00 each weekday. She would stay in this house, at least for now, but they would have to move sooner or later because she couldn't afford the rent for much longer unless she started working forty-plus hours a week.

She thought of these things as she drove home, despite telling herself she needed to stop thinking about the circumstances that brought them here. These thoughts were like a song she couldn't get out of her head, though. They seemed to have taken up permanent residence in her brain.

When she turned the key on the deadbolt of their front door, she was surprised not to feel the resistance of the lock being turned. Had she forgotten to lock the door that morning? She thought back but couldn't remember whether she had or not. Usually, such automatic actions didn't register in the mind, like turning off a running faucet or turning on a light when entering a dark room. It was something people did without thinking. Had her focus strayed that much that she didn't do something so basic as locking the door?

As she opened the door, she froze. What if the person who killed Brad had returned? What if he was in the house now?

Her heart ramming her ribs, she felt the urge to sleep scatter as adrenaline flooded her veins.

Slowly tiptoeing into the kitchen, she found it empty. She checked the other downstairs rooms. Empty. Not a thing out of place.

Stepping lightly up the stairs, taking care not to make a sound, she went first to the boys' rooms, checking them. Still nobody there. Had those who'd killed Brad come and gone already? She figured that would probably be the case since they would have worked out when she would be away from the house...unless they meant to kill her.

Her hand trembled as she turned the knob to enter her own room. Slowly, she eased the door open, cringing when the hinge protested lightly. Peeking into the room, she saw nothing at first. Again, nothing seemed out of place.

Then she saw Nick on her bed. For a moment, she thought of that creepy book and movie where the gangsters left a horse's head in the movie producer's bed. Had they killed Nick? Why was he there?

No longer caring if they were waiting in her

room, she rushed to the bed, already sobbing in her grief over what she worried had happened.

Kneeling beside her son's prostrate body, she reached out and shook him.

"Nick?"

No response from him caused a moment of panic. She shook him harder. "Nick!"

When he didn't move, she leaned over him, placing her ear to his chest. She heard his heart beating slowly. She knew people's heartbeat slowed when they slept, but this seemed unusually slow. There seemed to be at least a full second between beats, maybe more. She shook him again, this time hard enough for his head to roll back and forth on the pillow, following his shoulders as she pushed and pulled on him in an effort to wake him from this deepest level of sleep.

"NICK!" she shouted at him. "NICK, WAKE UP!"

When he didn't respond, she went to get a washcloth, intending to wet it with cold water and see if that helped revive her son. Grabbing the cloth from the small linen closet in her bathroom, she turned to the faucet and froze.

Her bottle of Ambien sat on the counter beside the sink, seeming to taunt her. She'd not used it last night, and she knew she always kept it in the medicine cabinet. That it had not been there that morning was not one of those 'did I or didn't I' wonderings. She always took the time to wipe down the counter after brushing her teeth, and if the bottle had been there, she would have seen it.

The sudden knowledge that Nick had attempted

suicide slammed her, making her heart ache as new tears filled her eyes. She knew he'd been depressed, as they all were, but she'd never thought anything close to this could happen. She figured her sons would work their way through the pain, as she was.

The sudden thought *Where is Jimmy?* crossed her mind. This was the last room she'd looked in while searching for intruders, so he wasn't here. She prayed he was still in school.

Apparently, Nick had not gone into the school building when she'd dropped him off that morning. He'd skipped school and come here to kill himself.

This thought rolled through her befuddled mind as she pulled out her phone and dialed 9-1-1.

Within fifteen minutes, both the police and two medics in an ambulance had arrived.

The medics began working on Nick. "Do you know when he might have taken the pills?"

"No. I figure he must have not gone into the school when I dropped him off this morning and came home."

The medic checked his watch. "That's been several hours, assuming he didn't go anywhere else."

"Will he be okay?"

"Not sure yet, ma'am. But if he took them hours ago, it doesn't appear he took enough to kill him. Do you know how many he took?"

"No."

The policeman was holding the bottle of Ambien and said, "The prescription is only two weeks old. Do you recall how many times you've taken one?"

She thought a moment, finally deciding. "Four. I've taken it four times."

"Did you ever take more than one?" the policeman asked.

"No."

He shook out the remaining pills and counted them. Looking at the medics, he said, "Six. He's taken six."

Holly watched the face of the medic facing her and felt some of the tension leave her shoulders when she saw him sigh and smile.

"Then definitely not enough to kill him, unless he has other medical conditions we don't know about." Looking at Holly, he asked, "Does your son have any known medical conditions? Heart problems? Asthma? Allergies to medications? Anything like that?"

"No," she answered. "Then he'll be alright?" she asked.

"Physically, yes, ma'am. But you have to remember he tried to take his life. He'll need counseling."

She rode in the ambulance with Nick. As they were on the way, she realized that Jimmy would be getting home to an empty house.

"My other son," she said. "He'll be home soon and not know what happened."

"Do you know someone to call?" the medic asked.

She considered this and was ashamed to admit she knew nobody well enough to make such a request of them. She suddenly felt very alone in the world.

"No."

"We can have the police pick him up and bring him to the emergency room," the medic said.

"Thank you." Holly sat back and did her best to hold in the panic that wanted to burst from her.

When the vehicle pulled into the ambulance bay at the Wharton Medical Center, they rushed Nick straight back to an exam room. They worked on Nick, giving him more drugs to counteract the Ambien.

After a while, he opened his eyes and looked around, appearing dazed and mostly unaware of his surroundings.

"Where am I?" he mumbled.

Holly leaned toward him. "You're in the emergency room at the hospital."

She could see the memory of what he'd done return, and his eyes filled with tears.

"Nick, honey, why? Why did you try to kill yourself?"

He shrugged and said nothing. Despite her best efforts to get him to open up to her, he refused to speak. Not to her. Not to anyone until Jimmy was ushered into the curtained cubicle. Then all he said was, "Get him out of here! I don't want him to see me like this!"

Holly considered refusing to send Jimmy away but didn't want to further upset Nick in his fragile state. Turning to Jimmy, she said, "Maybe it would be best if you waited in the waiting area."

Jimmy frowned at his brother and said, "Get better, Nick." Then he went through the curtain and out to the waiting room.

A nurse came in and told her they would be admitting Nick, which she'd expected. Hospitals did not send people who had attempted suicide home until they could be assured no further attempts would take place.

Holly finished up with the hospital's business office, including filling out the paperwork she needed to complete so they could admit Nick, thankful that Brad had paid for private insurance after leaving the firm in California.

24

I finally braved a phone call to Nick's house Tuesday evening. He'd not been in school since Friday, and I was afraid his family had left town. I prayed I wouldn't get one of those "this number has been disconnected" messages. Part of the reason I'd hesitated to call was fear of that message. If he moved, I knew I would never hear from him again. He hadn't answered my previous email, so I knew he wouldn't answer any others I sent. It would be like he'd disappeared from the face of the earth.

I was relieved when his little brother answered the phone. I couldn't remember his name.

"Hello?"

"Hi, is Nick home?"

Silence greeted me for a moment, then he said, "He's in the hospital."

I sat there, growing numb from the stunning news.

"What?"

"Yeah. He tried to kill himself. Took some of my mom's sleeping pills."

Tears burned my eyes.

"Really?"

"Yeah. They admitted him to the psych unit."

"Do you know what room he's in?"

"I don't remember, but they aren't letting anyone but family visit right now."

"Can he take a phone call?"

"I guess so."

"Sorry, but I forgot your name."

"Jimmy."

"Thanks, Jimmy. If you talk to him, tell him Maureen says hello in case I can't get in touch with him."

"Okay."

Hanging up, I sat on the bed in my room at the Turners'. I cried and did my best not to be too loud, but it didn't work. Jenny must have been walking by my room or something and heard me.

I heard a tap on my bedroom door followed by Jenny sticking her head in.

"Is everything okay?" she asked.

I wasn't sure how much of this I wanted to share. I was feeling ashamed that I hadn't said anything before. Maybe I could have prevented Nick from trying to kill himself, but I never thought he would try it even if he had said he'd been thinking about it. I couldn't come up with a plausible reason to be sitting on my bed crying without having a lie found out easily, which would harm the trust I'd built with Jack and Jenny, so I told her what had happened. I left out my own part in all this, though.

"Oh, my," Jenny said. My news had made her sad even though she didn't know Nick at all, and I knew that Jack would feel the same. It was a genuine sadness, not the typical response that sounded sad but really wasn't when the person didn't know the others involved.

Holding out her hand, she said, "Come with

me." She led me to their spacious living room where Jack was sitting on the sofa, reading.

"We need to talk about something," Jenny announced.

Jack looked up. He could see by my red eyes there was a problem. "What's wrong?"

Jenny sat on the sofa beside Jack and pointed to a chair that faced them for me to sit in. A mahogany sofa table stood between us.

Jenny waited for me to talk, so I said, "My best friend, Nick, tried to kill himself. He's in the hospital." It suddenly occurred to me how many people I was close to were in the hospital for various reasons, and I shuddered.

Later, when I had time to consider it, I came to the conclusion that stress is an odd thing. Sometimes, people are unaware of how much stress they're dealing with until later, but at that moment, I was completely aware of the level of stress in my life. My mother had nearly been killed in a traffic accident. My grandmother had suffered a heart attack that I'd been forced to deal with because I was the only other person there when it happened. Finally, my best friend had attempted suicide. All of this had happened in a matter of days. It was a wonder I wasn't joining Nick in the psych unit.

My mom had told me when something bad happened, I should count my blessings. Other than they were all alive—for now at least—I couldn't see any. Would my grandmother suffer a worse heart attack and die? Would the doctors find something else wrong with my mom that would mean she couldn't come home when she was scheduled to?

Would Nick get out of the hospital and succeed in killing himself? I had no idea what the answer was to any of these questions, and I didn't want to deal with them.

My brain was feeling fuzzy as if it was numb and I couldn't think straight, and I suppose that was more or less what was happening. They say stress is a killer. At that moment, I understood why.

I was having difficulty keeping up with the conversation due to that fuzzy-headed feeling. Jack was saying something, but I'd missed it.

"Huh?" I said.

Jack said, "Do you think Nick's mother would be okay with Jenny stopping in to speak to Nick in the hospital? She's a licensed therapist, you know."

"I don't know," I answered. "Do you want to talk to her about it?"

"Yes, I would," Jenny said.

"How much would it cost her?"

Jenny looked at me strangely and answered, "For your friend? Nothing."

Since my brain was completely in the moment because it couldn't think beyond that, I said, "Why did you look at me like that?"

"It was just an odd thing for you to say. Teenagers generally don't consider the costs, especially if it doesn't concern them and their family's finances."

"Oh," I said and leaned back against the chair. I was doing what my mother called "slouching," so I sat up straight again and scooted my butt back so I could lean into the chair's back.

"What's their number?" Jenny asked. It dawned

on me she meant to call Nick's mom right away.

"You're calling now?"

"Yes. No time like the present, as they say."

I felt life was moving at light speed. "Can't it wait until tomorrow?" I wasn't sure why I didn't want Jenny to talk to Nick or his mom tonight, but it seemed to have something to do with my part in all of this, as if maybe Nick's mom had talked to Nick, and he'd told her it was all my fault for creating an email address for him.

I burst into tears and ran to my bedroom.

Of course, Jenny followed a moment later.

"What's wrong, hon? Why don't you want me to call Nick's mom?"

"I don't know," I whined. It was as honest an answer as I could give. I sort of understood why, but then again, I didn't. I changed the subject, or at least I thought I did.

"My life's a mess! Everyone in my family and my best friend are in the hospital! It's like I'm being punished!" That thought led to thoughts of my part in what happened to Nick. Maybe I *was* being punished.

"Honey, what do you have to be punished for? It's not your fault that all this has happened. I know you're under a lot of stress because of the changes in your life, but none of it is your fault."

"Yes it is."

"How?"

The tears suddenly eased with the reality that I was about to confess my part in what had happened to Nick and his father. It was strangely soothing.

"What happened to Nick and his father might

be my fault," I said.

"Don't be silly, honey. How could any of it be your fault?"

I explained to her about the email I had set up for Nick and that he had emailed a friend in California. I told her about Nick being sure his email had been intercepted by the people who had been searching for Nick's dad. Of course, none of this about how Nick's family was running from someone who wanted Nick's father dead had come out in the news. Nick's mom may have told the police, but they hadn't shared that with the press.

Jenny listened to me, her mouth almost hanging open she was so shocked.

When I'd finished, she said, "This is why you think Nick tried to kill himself? Because he blames himself for his father's murder?"

I nodded.

"Honey?"

"Yeah?"

"Are you thinking about doing anything like that, too?"

I shook my head in complete denial of even thinking about it. "No!" I said. "I would never do that!"

She put her hand on my hair and stroked it. Her touch felt like an angel's.

"Sweetheart, if you ever do think about that, promise me you'll talk to me about it. Suicide is never the answer."

"I know. I won't think about doing anything like that, but if I do, I promise I'll talk to you."

I was already feeling guilty that I'd said

nothing before now about Nick and what he'd told me in the school arboretum that day. Of course, if I killed myself, I wouldn't feel any guilt that I'd not said anything to Jenny or anyone else, but I knew it would hurt her deeply if that happened, not to mention my family.

I gave her the phone number to Nick's house. She leaned down and kissed my hairline. It was something my mom used to do when I was little, and it made me want to cry again, but I didn't. Like her touch, her kiss was like an angel's.

My heart filled with so much love for her that I quickly sat up in bed and threw my arms around her neck, holding her tightly against me as she patted my back and stroked my hair.

25

Jenny left me and I lay there thinking about how much better I felt now that I'd told someone about what I'd done. It was like I was sharing the weight of knowing and it wasn't so heavy anymore.

I finally went back to the main room. Jack and Jenny were talking.

"I just got off the phone with Nick's mother," Jenny said. "She would love for me to come see Nick."

"But he can't have visitors unless its family," I said.

Jenny smiled. "They'll let me see him because I'll be seeing him in my professional capacity as a therapist."

"Oh." Then I thought of something. "Can I go with you when you talk to him?"

"I'm afraid not, hon. First, what we say is private. Second, they still won't let people who aren't related to him in to see him, even if you're with me."

"Will you tell him I said hello?"

"Of course," she said. "And Ms. Winslow doesn't want this news spread at school," she said.

After dinner, I took my shower and went to bed. I thought about trying to call Nick, but I didn't think I would get through because I didn't know his room number.

I would have to tell Mia and Cameron about Nick. I couldn't exactly keep that to myself. If they found out I knew he'd tried to kill himself and didn't say anything, they would hate me. I would swear them to secrecy. I hoped that would work. I knew Cameron was good at keeping a secret, unlike most of the kids I knew. Mia, though, was a gamble. I prayed she could keep it to herself.

The next morning as we sat at our usual table in the cafeteria, I said, "I have some news about Nick, but you have to swear—and I mean really swear— that you won't tell anyone else. The only reason I'm telling you is that we were all his first friends here. Maybe his only friends."

Mia tried to pretend she didn't care, but I knew she did. She'd had different boyfriends since she was nine, and she'd always been the one to end the relationship. Having a guy leave her was something new, and I think she was still adjusting to the idea.

"I won't say anything because I really don't care, whatever it is," she said. "He's dead to me."

Wow. I hoped she didn't regret those words after I told her what had happened. The look on my face must have told her what a terrible thing it was to say that.

"What do you expect, Maureen? He left me!"

"No, that's not it exactly, it's just—"

"Just what?"

"Nick tried to commit suicide."

Both girls' jaws dropped open and their eyes went wide. Then they both teared up.

"Oh my...oh...." Mia said. "I didn't mean that, Maureen. You know I didn't mean it. Not like that."

"I know."

"Why?" Cameron asked. She had the look of someone who had just heard news she considered an impossibility, as if I'd just said the Turners' dog had sprouted wings and flown.

"I don't know," I lied before correcting myself. "Well, he did think he was responsible for his father's murder."

Cameron said, "What? How could he be responsible?"

I could see this leading to another confession, and I didn't want the world to know what I'd done, so I told them about the email he'd sent his friend in California without mentioning my role.

Mia said, "So he thinks they found out where his family was from the email?"

I nodded.

Soon, Cameron and Mia were crying, and that made me cry, too.

Ms. Henderson, my English teacher, saw us and came over.

"What's wrong, girls?"

"Nick Winslow tried to kill himself," Mia blurted, loud enough to be heard several tables away. I instantly knew the news would be all over the school before the tardy bell rang for first class. I felt shame mix with my sorrow as I realized this.

Ms. Henderson said, "Come with me" and turned toward the hallway leading to the front office.

We followed, three sobbing girls afraid for their friend. I was surprised when we walked past the main office, but realized where we were going when she opened the door to the guidance office.

We sat crying in the small waiting area, and Ms. Henderson went back to talk to a counselor. A minute later, she was back and told us to follow her again.

We entered Ms. McGuire's office, the lead guidance counselor at the school. She gave us a sad smile as we sat, and Ms. Henderson left us with her.

Ms. McGuire was near Jenny's age, in her mid-fifties, and had salt and pepper hair that was arranged neatly in coils atop her head. She was a kind woman, as counselors tended to be, and her look of sadness told us she truly cared.

"So you've heard?" she began.

"You knew?" I asked.

"Yes, of course. We just didn't feel it was something that should be shared with the students if they didn't know. That's not something we advertise at the school. There's a stigma that follows students who attempt suicide, and we'd hoped to avoid that. Can I ask who told you?"

Mia and Cameron looked at me, and Cameron said, "Maureen told us."

Ms. McGuire turned to me and said, "How did you find out?"

"I called to talk to Nick last night. His little brother told me."

She sat back. "Ahh, that explains it. His mother didn't want everyone knowing. I guess she forgot to tell her younger son not to say anything."

"Ms. McGuire?" I said.

"Yes?"

"I think maybe some people in the cafeteria

heard us mention it." I didn't want to mention Mia's outburst. She hadn't meant to tell the world.

Ms. McGuire understood immediately. It would be all over the school very soon. It's possible the entire cafeteria knew by the time we sat down in these chairs. News like that moves at light speed.

"Well, then, I suppose we'll have to have another assembly. We'll want everyone being nice to Nick when he finally returns to school. Bad treatment would only make it worse." She thought for a moment and said, "Stay here."

She stepped out of her office, and a few minutes later she returned with Mr. Lance. He didn't look happy.

"Ms. Winslow didn't want the students to know this," he said.

I ducked my head, ashamed that I'd been the one to set this uncontrolled fire. I hadn't counted on outbursts being overheard.

After Mr. Lance had the full details of how it came about that the entire school would be aware of what had happened, he looked at me. "Maureen, did you know this news was supposed to be kept away from the student body?"

I nodded. "Yes, sir."

He sighed. "I'll deal with you later, then. It seems I have another assembly to put together before the end of first period."

He was angry, and misery washed over me that I would be the one to incur the results of his wrath.

Twenty minutes later, we were herded into the auditorium for an assembly. It was easy to see that everyone knew why this one was happening. The news had spread. When I'd entered class with my pass from Guidance, heads had turned to me. Some of the eyes asked silently if I had heard. My own look told them I had.

By the time I went to lunch, all the teachers seemed to know who had brought the news into the public eye. I guess teachers had their own grapevine that was kept from the kids' ears. I could picture them in the teachers' lounge.

"Did you hear it was Maureen Lindstrom who brought the news into the school? And after Nick's mother had gone to such lengths to keep it quiet!"

Of course, that was only my imagination, but I doubted it was far from the truth.

That afternoon, Mr. Lance called me into the office. As I sat waiting for him to drop the bomb on me, I considered what I'd done wrong. Yes, I had told Mia and Cameron, but that anyone else knew was purely an accident.

Once I was seated in Mr. Lance's office, I tried to explain that. In fact, I launched into my explanation without waiting for him to speak, hoping I could forego the lecture if he realized I had meant no harm.

As I burst into the details, he held his hand up in a stop gesture.

"I have no intention of punishing you," he said. "I just want to talk to you about the importance of keeping secrets that should be kept. While it's true that some people will tell you not to say anything to anyone else about certain matters, and you should not listen to them, it is equally true that if there is no good reason to tell a secret, especially one that could end up harming someone else, you should honor that request. Ms. Henderson explained that you probably thought you could tell your two friends and that would be all, but the truth is these things rarely stay quiet once someone knows. Ms. McGuire told me you learned about this from Nick's younger brother, is that right?"

"Yes, sir."

"Well, it is what it is, and we'll have to deal with it. Do you think my admonition to the students today will prevent people from harassing Nick when he returns?"

"I think so."

"Well, I certainly hope so. I pretty well threatened them with the severest penalty I could give if it was reported that Nick was being harassed or bullied over this." He changed the subject. "You're Nick's friend, right?"

"Yes, sir."

"Then as his friend, you will need to watch out and see to it that nobody says anything to Nick about this in any way that might hurt Nick's feelings. If you see something like that, immediately tell a teacher or come to the office and tell me or another administrator. Am I clear?"

"Yes, sir."

He looked at me for a moment and said, "You can get a pass back to class from Ms. Rehnquist. Just be sure you don't tell secrets you shouldn't tell from now on. Okay?"

"Yes, sir."

When I returned to class, I did my best to ignore everyone. The last bell would ring soon to send us home. It had been a terrible day.

As I rode home on the bus, I wondered when I would be able to visit my mom and grandmother again. We'd not visited since Sunday, and this was Wednesday. I found it kind of weird that I missed it, considering how much I had hated it before.

Arriving at my temporary home, I used the key to let myself in. Then I went out back to visit Bluebelle, but she wasn't there. I figured Jack had taken her to work with him that day, so I just did my homework and watched TV until Jenny got home.

When she arrived, she sat beside me. "I talked to Nick today."

"What did he say?"

"Not much, actually, until I told him of our conversation."

This surprised me. "I didn't think you'd tell him I told you!" I was suddenly reminded of what Mr. Lance had said about secrets.

"Honey, I had to tell him I knew. He wouldn't have said anything if I hadn't. Besides, he would have told me eventually himself."

"He'll be mad at me."

"He wasn't mad. I told him you told me because you care about him, and he seemed to accept that."

"Then he's not mad?"

"No."

I was curious about something. "Do you think he'll try it again?"

"I doubt it, but who knows? It's too soon to tell. He's still devastated that his father is dead and he feels responsible. I tried to steer him to understand it wasn't his fault, but so far he's not listening to that. It will take time, but I think he'll be okay."

"Jenny?"

"Yes?"

"When can we go see my mom and grandma?"

"How about tomorrow after school? I can be here soon after you get home and finish your homework."

"That sounds good." Then I knew I had to tell Jenny what happened in school today. "Jenny?"

"Yes?"

"I messed up today."

"How?"

"You see, I knew I had to tell Mia and Cameron about Nick. They would hate me if I knew and said nothing. Anyway, when I did, Mia sort of burst out with what happened, and soon it was all over school. Mr. Lance had another assembly and threatened everyone within an inch of their lives if they were mean to Nick when he returned."

She looked at me for a moment, then said, "I can understand why you told them, but you realize you shouldn't have because his mom didn't want it all over school, right?"

"Yes."

"I'm sure Mr. Lance probably called Ms. Winslow and told her about this, but I think you need to phone her and apologize."

I didn't like that idea while knowing she was right. It's weird how often what's right isn't the easy thing to do.

"Okay. When should I call?"

"As I like to say, no time like the present."

Heaving a deep sigh, I took her phone as she held it out to me. "Her home phone number is in my contacts," Jenny said.

I opened her contacts and found the number. I pressed the entry, and the phone connected. When Ms. Winslow answered, I said, "Ms. Winslow? It's Maureen Lindstrom."

Her tone told me she knew why I was calling. "Maureen." I waited for her to yell at me, but she didn't. Instead, there was silence for a moment before she said, "Mr. Lance called me today. Why did you tell someone?"

"I didn't mean for it to get all over school. It's just that Mia reacted badly about it, and blurted the news out. I'm so sorry."

"But why tell Mia at all?"

"Well, she was his girlfriend, and if she found out I knew, she'd hate me for not telling her."

Ms. Winslow sighed. "I guess it would have gotten out eventually anyway. I was just hoping to save Nick the grief the kids will give him over this."

"I don't think they'll do that. Mr. Lance was very stern about how we were to treat Nick when he comes back to school."

"Okay," she said. "I remember what it was like to be thirteen, and while it was the wrong thing to do, what's done is done."

"You're not angry with me?"

"No, dear. I'm not happy about it, but being mad at you won't make things better. Nick needs a friend when he comes home, and although you made this mistake, I know you care about him."

She could hear that I was crying and said, "It's okay, hon. Just help Nick when he comes home."

"I will. Thank you for understanding that I didn't mean for this to get out."

"You're welcome."

We ended the call, and I handed Jenny her phone.

"Everything's okay?"

I nodded, and she smiled at me. "The conversation wasn't as bad as you thought it would be, was it?"

"No."

"Remember that. Things are never as good or as bad as we think they will be."

I smiled back at her, returning to watch the program on TV to get my mind off what happened, and Jenny got up to start fixing dinner.

26

By the time I finished my homework the following day, Jenny walked through the door, asking if I was ready to visit Mom and Grandma. I had looked forward to this as much as I dreaded it before.

"Ready," I said, putting away my school books.

As we drove, I asked if she'd seen Nick.

"I figured I would go see him while you were with your mom," she said. "Your mom doesn't know about him, right?"

"No."

"Do you think you should talk to her about it?"

"I will." I had intended to do that without her suggesting it.

When we arrived at Mom's room, Jenny talked with her for a few minutes. Jenny didn't mention Nick. Apparently, she was letting me do that.

Looking at me, Jenny said, "When you're done talking with your mom, you can go see your grandmother. I'll meet you at her room in about an hour, okay?"

"Okay," I said.

After Jenny left, I said, "Mom? You remember my friend Nick?"

"Yes."

Suddenly, I didn't know how to put what I had to say in words. It wasn't something a person blurted out, but I could think of no other way to say it. I paused long enough that mom said, "So what about him? Did he ask you out on a date?"

"No. He tried to commit suicide."

Her face was still bandaged where she'd been cut in the wreck, but I could see her expression change. Her color went pale and her eyes widened slightly. "What?!"

"Yeah, he took some of his mom's sleeping pills."

"Why would he do something like that?"

Okay, here was the real reason Jenny wanted me to talk to Mom about Nick. She knew Mom would ask that question, and I was a bit taken aback that I'd not realized that.

Caught without a lie to cover my involvement, I stammered, "I don't know." Mom's ability to see a lie coming told her I wasn't telling the truth. I doubted it was very hard to do that. I could feel my face blushing.

"Yes, you do. Tell me."

I took a deep breath and said, "Okay, but you have to understand I didn't realize this would happen, okay?"

"Okay." She waited for me to continue.

Taking another breath, I told her about getting Nick the email address and how he decided his email to his friend had been used to find them.

She took this in, thought about it, and said, "His parents didn't want him emailing friends?"

"Uh-huh."

"But you helped him set up an email address anyway?"

"Yes."

"Honey, you couldn't have known this would happen, but you helped a friend disobey his parents. I know it seemed minor at the time, but neither of you understood why his parents made that rule. We don't just come up with rules to upset our kids."

"I know."

"You had nothing to do with what Nick did. That was his decision. He could have created the email himself, but from what you tell me, it was more your idea, right?"

"Yeah. That's why I feel so bad about it."

"I'm not upset because what you did contributed to Nick's suicide attempt since it didn't have anything to do with it, really. As I said, that was Nick's decision, and he could have created an email address behind his parents' backs without you. My problem is that you helped someone disobey his parents. That was wrong."

"I know."

"Have you told your grandmother yet?"

"No."

"Well, her health isn't good right now. A heart is a funny thing. Bad news like this won't help her at all. So, I want you to wait until she's better to tell her about Nick."

"Then I don't have to tell her?" This was good news.

"You will, just not now. Let's wait until she's out of the woods with her heart. It's my understanding they're putting in a stent tomorrow."

"You talked to her?"

"Yes, but I also get news from her doctor.

She's allowed him talk to me about her condition."

"You mean he comes by to talk to you?"

She held up her phone. "No, his office emails me everything going on with her."

"Oh." That made sense. I couldn't imagine a doctor coming up to Mom's room to talk to her about Grandma, though I guess it could happen. I just always thought doctors would be too busy to do that kind of thing.

We chatted a little longer before I went to see Grandma. Based on when Jenny left the room, I would have only about fifteen minutes with her, which suited me.

Entering her room, I found Grandma sitting and watching a game show on TV. Her dinner had just been delivered.

"What? How did you get here?" she asked.

"Jenny brought me to talk to you and Mom."

"So you've seen your mother?"

"Yes."

I hugged her and asked how she was feeling (*fine, thank you*), and she launched into complaints about the food. It didn't look that bad to me, but she said, "It's tasteless, really. No salt at all. Not a bit."

My grandmother really liked salt on her food. Too much was a bad thing for anyone, but I figured with her heart, it was especially bad.

"You can't eat salt anymore, Grandma. It's bad for your heart."

She looked at me. "You're telling me what I can and can't do?"

She was obviously in a bad mood, and I suddenly couldn't wait for Jenny to get there.

"No, Grandma. I'm just saying if you want your heart to get better, you should eat less salt."

"Why do you care? It's my heart."

I couldn't believe she said that. I stared at her. "Because I love you and don't want to lose you, especially since we've started getting to know each other better. I haven't had enough time with you yet."

Her look softened. "Okay. I'm sorry."

Changing the subject, she said, "How's school going?"

"Fine. I have a quiz on Friday in math, and I'll be doing some extra studying when I get home."

"How do you like staying with the Turners?"

I grinned. "A lot. They're really nice people, and they have a dog named Bluebelle."

"I know about Bluebelle. Jack Turner does love his dogs."

"Do you think I might be able to talk Mom into letting me get one when she gets home?"

"I don't know. You can try."

We continued talking about various things while Grandma ignored her dinner. About ten minutes after I got there, Jenny came in.

She and Grandma talked while Jenny more or less force-fed Grandma her food. I couldn't have done that, of course, but Jenny was able to while Grandma protested mildly about the bland taste.

"It's not the taste that matters at this point," Jenny said. "You have to get your nourishment if you expect to go home soon."

"I'm having a stent put in my heart tomorrow," Grandma said. "That alone makes me not want to eat anything tonight."

Jenny smiled and nodded. "Be that as it may, you have to keep your strength up."

On the ride home, I talked to Jenny about what my mom said and why she was upset that I created the email account for Nick. Then I asked her, "What did Nick say when you talked to him?"

She glanced my way with a smile. "I can't tell you, hon. It's confidential."

I'd seen enough cop shows to know about how private doctor-patient information was, but for some reason it hadn't occurred to me that Jenny would be bound by it with Nick. He was my best friend.

"You can't tell me anything he said?"

"Well, there is one thing because he wanted me to tell you something."

"What?"

"He said not to blame yourself for what happened."

I sat back in my seat and thought about that. "Can you tell me anything that you said to him?"

"Not really, no. But what he wanted me to tell you is important. He's right. You have enough to worry about without blaming yourself for what Nick decided to do on his own."

"Mom told me that, too, at least the part about not blaming myself."

"Jack and I said the same thing," she said. "I guess it must be true, then, if that many people have told you that in the last twenty-four hours."

"I guess so," I said.

"How did your visits with your mom and grandma go?" she asked.

I told her about my time with them as we rode along. When we got home, she told me she needed to start dinner, and I did a little extra studying for my math quiz. Math was not my best subject, and I needed all the preparation I could get.

27

After a week went by, a lot had changed. My mom had been moved to the rehab center to work on getting herself back to where she could walk and do most of what she could before. Grandma had been moved to what was called an elder care facility. She would live there for now, at least until Mom was able to come home. The visiting hours at these places were more flexible than the hospital's.

Mom had put Grandma's house on the market when she moved in, and it sold. The money from that would be in Grandma's bank account by the end of the month, and she would use that money to pay her monthly rent at the place where she now lived.

Needless to say, Grandma hated it. Jenny or Jack would take me there to visit, and I didn't really blame her. It was a nice place, but it was also kind of depressing, not to mention her meals were still bland. She couldn't come home because Mom didn't want me being responsible for her. That bothered me because I felt I could take care of Grandma if something happened—I'd done it once, hadn't I? But it also didn't bother me because it meant I could stay with the Turners.

One day when Jenny got home, she asked if I wanted to see Nick.

"Of course!" I said.

Nick had been moved out of the psych unit into a place for kids with depression issues. I don't know how Ms. Winslow felt about that, but I imagine she was about as happy with the arrangement as Grandma was with hers.

Jenny said Nick's mom had given her permission to talk to me about Nick and his condition. When I asked how Nick felt about that, she said, "He was okay with it." I didn't know at the time how much she was shading her answer. I found out when I saw him the first time.

He was watching TV at the facility where he was staying when I walked in with Jenny. I wanted to run over and hug him but didn't. A few people were sitting around, and I didn't want them to think he was my boyfriend or anything.

I grinned at him as I walked up, but he more or less ignored me. I felt my grin melt as I got closer.

Jenny said, "How are you today, Nick?"

"Fine."

He didn't look fine. He looked ready to try suicide again. That's when I noticed that while he was looking at the TV, he didn't seem to really be watching it.

The show was an old western from way back when TV was mostly new. I'd seen a few of them before but didn't really like them much. They were mostly the same. Tough guys working on ranches and Native Americans typically shown as either stupid, mean, or downright evil. You also always knew the ranch's cook because he was the smallest man on the show. The only women were mostly wives taking care of the house. Doctors were always old, and women were always pretty and wore dresses, which seemed kind of odd for people choosing to live such a rough life. They wouldn't dare put a woman on the ranch or give her any responsibility back then. Such backward times!

Anyway, I said, "Whatcha watching?" I thought it might be a good conversation starter.

"Some western."

He'd always been a quiet kind of person, but this was beyond anything I'd ever seen from him.

I looked at Jenny for a suggestion on what I could do or say, but she just shrugged and nodded to the place on the sofa next to where Nick was sitting. Then she said, "I'll leave you two alone to catch up." Then she turned and walked down a nearby hallway. I had no idea what was down there, but I figured she did.

I sat down, and Nick barely acknowledged me. He glanced my way before turning back to the program he wasn't really watching.

"Nick?" I could hear the tears wanting to come from deep inside me.

He turned his gaze dully toward me. I waited for him to speak, figuring that would be at least some acknowledgement of my desire to talk to him.

"Yeah?"

"Didn't you say it was okay for me to come visit you?"

"They asked if I wanted to see you, and I shrugged. I guess they took that for a yes. Mostly, though, to be honest, I don't care."

That cut deep. I couldn't help it. The tears

began to flow. I sat there crying as Nick ignored me as well as the program on TV. I would have preferred he chose the TV over me, but basically, he was choosing an emptiness over me. Some place in his head that was a void of thought or feeling. That was much worse.

"Nick? Talk to me. Please?"

He turned back to me. "Why are you here?"

"Because you're my friend and I'm worried about you," I said.

"Well, don't be."

"Don't be worried about you? I can't help that. You're my friend. My best friend."

"I meant it both ways. Don't be my friend either."

I sat there, wondering at the amount of pain he felt that he didn't want me to be his friend. Did he blame me that much? I had to know.

"Nick, do you blame me for what happened?"

He seemed to consider it before answering. "No. I probably would have created an email account myself in time. That wouldn't have changed anything that happened."

"You can't be sure they found you because of your email."

He stared at me, his face lacking any emotion beyond his depression.

"Nick, it's not your fault your dad is dead."

Suddenly, the person who'd been sitting there without any emotion at all was angry.

"My dad's not dead!" he said, almost a whisper. "Why won't everyone stop saying that?! My dad's not DEAD!" His voice had quickly risen

221

to a shout by the last word.

I was stunned. I'd heard about people sometimes choosing to ignore a fact if it made them sad enough. It had been in an article about depression I'd read once for school. Deep down, the people knew they were lying to themselves but refused to acknowledge that truth. Still, I was shocked. We had talked about his father's death before, but now he was denying it happened. The fact he was denying it seemed as if I'd suddenly crossed into some kind of other dimension, like in the old TV show *Twilight Zone*. One second, Nick was talking about his father's death. The next second, he was denying his father was dead. Weird was not sufficient to describe it.

I wanted to ask Nick what was going on, but I knew I couldn't. This would take someone with more experience dealing with such feelings. Someone like Jenny.

Nick's voice returned to normal, and he told me to leave, but not in those words. He'd actually told me to get the you-know-what away from him, and his use of the only cuss word so bad it was referred to by its first letter shocked me, too. He'd never used language like that around me.

I was so stunned by our brief conversation that I wasn't even crying anymore. I stood up, deciding to grant his wish but also deciding to tell him how I felt.

"Okay, I'll leave you alone, but remember this. I love you, Nick. Not like a boyfriend, but as a friend. You and your life mean a lot to me. You mean a lot to a lot of people. Stick around long enough to figure that out, okay?"

I turned and walked away but not before noticing that it was obvious he'd heard me. His expression changed slightly, as if maybe he was sorry he'd been mean to me. I don't know if that's what happened, but at least there was a response other than anger.

I walked down the hallway where Jenny had gone and found her in a small lounge area with vending machines. She was drinking a cup of coffee and reading something on her phone. When she saw me, she could tell it hadn't gone well.

"Oh, dear. I'm sorry. What happened?"

I told her everything, including his parting words to me, but using the first letter of the cuss word he'd used.

She hugged me and asked me to sit beside her. "I was hoping that seeing a friend would help him talk. Sometimes he's in denial about his father's death. Other times, he can talk about it. He'll come out of that. He knows his father is dead, but sometimes, out of the blue, he'll deny it. It's his way of coping with it at this point."

"Do you think Nick will ever want to see me again?"

"Yes, but later, when he's more ready. I'd hoped seeing you would make him happy. I'm sorry. I guess I was wrong."

When we went back through the main room where Nick had been sitting, he was gone. We went home, stopping for frozen yogurt on the way. I figured it was Jenny's way of trying to make me feel better about what had happened, but it didn't.

28

Holly Winslow stared at the bank statement. Brad had rented a safe deposit box before his murder that left her a widow. Brad had always handled the family's finances. As an accountant, that was only natural. Forced now to deal with everything from paying bills to balancing the checkbook, she had found the inclusion of a monthly charge for a safe deposit box on the bank statement. Now, she wondered what could be in there.

They had no valuables to speak of beyond her engagement ring, which probably wasn't worth more than a couple of thousand dollars at the most. They had nothing of value that would require certificates. They rented the home in Denton where they lived, so there wouldn't even be mortgage documents.

The thought of what might be in the safe deposit box frightened her. She knew no details of what he'd found that incriminated his former boss in California, but now she wondered if he'd kept copies of the proof, whatever it was. If he had, he certainly wouldn't have kept such documents in their home.

She had come home one day after his murder and found the house ransacked. She'd said nothing to the boys and cleaned up the mess because she didn't want them to see it. That would have frightened them. Nothing was missing from the home, not even the few pieces of jewelry that were of some value. That suggested they hadn't been there to steal anything. They'd been looking for something. Nick was already worried that whoever killed his father might come after the rest of them. Seeing a ransacked house would have only heightened those fears. She had done her best not to let it send her into a panic.

When she'd found the house had been ransacked, she had arranged for a friend to let the boys stay overnight, using the excuse she had a lot of things to do as a result of Brad's death that she could more easily accomplish without the boys. She'd used that night and the following day while the boys were away to clean up the mess. She hadn't bothered to notify the police, since that would lead to the boys finding out what happened, and she doubted these people would have left any prints. Whoever had killed Brad was a professional. Professionals left no clues behind, especially something as simple as fingerprints.

Her mind returned to the possibility that Brad had rented the box to store proof of the crime. That was what he would have done if he had such proof. Now, she wondered if she even wanted to see whatever was in the bank's vault. Her name was on the bank account, so she assumed she would be able to get in to examine the contents. If she decided to look at whatever was in there and it turned out to be what she suspected, she would be in danger herself. If she didn't, she would always wonder.

The box would have to be emptied someday, of course. She didn't want to continue paying for a safe deposit box in a bank in Denton, Florida, especially if she decided to move away and start a new life for herself and the boys.

She wondered where Brad's key to the box would be. Upon considering this, she remembered tossing Brad's keys into the junk drawer in their kitchen when she'd received his personal effects from the mortuary that had cremated his body. She stood and walked into the kitchen, pulling the drawer open and rummaging through the contents.

Finding his keys, she fumbled through them until she found what she figured had to be the key to the safe deposit box. It was the only one she didn't recognize, and its head was different from any key she'd seen before.

Feeling her breathing become gasps, she closed her eyes and concentrated on calming herself. Panic would serve no purpose.

As she thought this, she realized that if incriminating documents of some sort were in the box she was running into danger, not away from it.

She sat thinking about this for over an hour, alternating between the answers *yes* and *no* to the question of whether she should check the contents of the box or not.

Finally, she considered her sons. As long as these people who had committed this horrible crime were able to get away with it, she and the boys would be forced to live in fear.

Fear or some other overwhelming emotion had already nearly taken Nick from her. If she could show that the ones responsible for their father's death had faced justice, perhaps they could all live with themselves. Perhaps Nick could get over the feelings of remorse or shame that had led him to attempt suicide.

Grabbing her purse, she left the house with Brad's keys.

After speaking with someone at the bank, she was escorted back to the area of the vault containing the safe deposit boxes. The bank employee inserted the bank's key, and she inserted Brad's. Soon, she had the box open after being left alone where she could view its contents.

She froze as she looked inside. Lying on top of a stack of papers she found an envelope with her name on it. The handwriting was Brad's, and seeing it made her heart skip.

With trembling fingers, she opened the envelope and withdrew the single sheet of paper. It was written by hand, not typed or printed, in Brad's handwriting.

Holly,

Forgive the dramatic cliché, but if you're reading this, I am either dead, missing, or in a coma. If I'm missing, I'm sorry, but I'm probably dead and my body won't be found.

I told you I had discovered evidence of serious crimes committed by my former boss, David Bender, but I refused to share the information with you for fear it would endanger your life. You may still be in danger, and if you're still in the town where whatever happened to cause you to be here now occurred, you should seriously consider moving as soon as possible.

Bender is extremely evil. You're probably being watched, and the phones are likely tapped as well.

In this box are documents that will prove the crimes Bender has committed, which are extensive. Since you will only be knowing about this safe deposit box if something has happened to me, then you must take steps to see that Bender and the rest are arrested and tried for their crimes.

I won't go into the details of their crimes, but it involves billions of dollars and possibly murders beyond my own. If I can figure that out from these documents, so can the police in California.

Bender only knows that I know what happened. I sent him an email stating that I would never tell anyone about it, including you. However, if I am dead, all bets are off.

Take these documents, along with this letter, and give it to an attorney, who will forward it to a dependable cop. Don't deliver them to the police yourself. I'm sure there are some working for the federal government who are on Bender's payroll. In fact, these documents prove that as well.

To be honest, I doubted we would be successful in our efforts to hide, and what has happened turned out to be only a matter of time, whether or not I turned over the copies of the documents that are in this box to the police. I just didn't want Bender to harm you. That's why I kept the documents instead of turning them in to the police. I had hoped it was some kind of leverage. Now that I'm likely dead since you're reading this, I think it would be best to do what I suggest in this letter. Again, do NOT take it directly to the police. Let a lawyer do that. He or she will know someone honest.

Please know that if you say anything to anyone other than an attorney in their private office about what is in here, you will be in very grave danger. I would even check out the attorney before going to speak to them. Also, be sure these documents are hidden away in your purse before leaving the bank. Nobody should see you with them, not even in the bank's lobby.

I love you with every fiber of my being.

Brad ^

Tears clouded her vision as she read. When they were first dating, he would always sign his notes to her with the small caret mark. It was his way of saying, "Look up! Nothing is as bad as it seems."

She took out the small stack of documents and looked at them. Many were copies of ledger sheets, and she could make nothing of them. However, quite a few entries were marked with an asterisk that had been added in red ink after making the copy. She supposed these were some of the expenditures that were evidence of a crime. She figured an accountant might know why her husband had flagged certain entries. Perhaps they'd been paying people off or making shady investments? She didn't know. She did know that some companies did what was called, "cooking the books," and this was probably something that might be traced to that in some way. But she wasn't sure why such "cooking" would result in the murder of her husband.

She stuffed the papers into her purse. After the safe deposit box was replaced, she left the bank and went home. She needed to find an attorney she could trust.

29

The next morning as I got ready for school, Jenny suggested I write Nick a letter, telling him how much I hoped he would get better and being honest with him about how I felt.

"Be totally honest and don't worry if he doesn't want to hear what you have to say. More important, don't be embarrassed by anything you say in the letter about how you feel. If you love him, tell him."

"I love him, but only as my best friend," I said.

"Then tell him that."

"But he knows already."

"It doesn't hurt to hear it again once in a while. What if your mother only told you she loved you once and never said it again?"

Okay, she'd made her point.

"Do you think it will help?"

"I don't know, but it's worth a try. Besides, you'll feel better knowing you tried again."

I ate my breakfast and thought about what I would write. Then, Jenny said, "Have you spoken to his mother since you apologized to her?"

"No."

"Maybe you should call and tell her you're thinking of them. It would be a nice gesture."

When I got home from school, I did my homework and then took out a sheet of paper. I stared at it for a while, trying to remember all the points I'd made in my head that morning that I wanted to say in my letter. I really wanted this to work. I knew it wouldn't solve the entire mess, but it would be a start if he would just talk to me. After thinking about how to begin, I started the letter.

Dear Nick,

I can't tell you how sorry I am that this has happened. Nobody deserves to lose a father. And don't think to yourself that he isn't dead. We both know he is. Jenny said when you got angry and said that, it was just you trying to cope with your loss. Anyway, I almost lost my mom in a car accident a couple of weeks ago, and just nearly losing her almost made me panic. Then my grandma had a heart attack, and I was the only person at home to call 9-1-1. I was scared out of my mind. What if I lost both of them? Because of this happening to me, I can't imagine what you felt like when your dad was killed. It had to be a hundred times worse because at least my mom and grandma survived. I don't think I've said this to you before. Maybe I have, but I want you to know that I love you. Not LOVE love. Just best friend love. You're very important to me, and I miss talking with you and seeing you. I looked forward to seeing you when I came there yesterday. Jenny said I could, and I was so excited. Then you didn't want to talk to me. I don't want to make you mad, but you really hurt my feelings. I'd sort of imagined that you would smile real big when you saw I'd come to visit you. I was really hurt that you barely said anything, and you acted like you wanted me to go away and die. I know others have said this, including me, but I'll say it again. None of this is your fault. Even if they did find you from your email, it's not your fault. It's theirs. The people who sent someone to kill your dad. They didn't need to do that. If there was a problem, they should have just talked it out. Jack and Jenny say talking out your problems makes them hurt less and sometimes you find a solution when you talk them out with someone. If you don't want to talk them out with me, at least talk them out with Jenny. She's a nice person and really cares about people. My mom once told me that if we didn't care about other people, we wouldn't feel hurt by them. Then she said that being hurt was worth it. That going through life alone is the saddest life there is. You're not alone, Nick. You have your mom, your brother, Jenny, me, and a lot of other people. We all care about you. Imagine how we'd feel if something happened and you weren't here anymore. Sure, you wouldn't be in pain from your dad's death anymore, but where would that leave the rest of us? Killing yourself isn't the answer, and neither is shutting everyone out. I want to come see you again, but if you don't want that, I won't. But I think talking to me and accepting my friendship will go a long way to helping you feel better because we all need friends, and we all need them to show they care. Just let Jenny know if you will see me. If not, I understand, though it will hurt.

Love,

Maureen

I read over my letter. It was all one paragraph, which would have made Ms. Henderson have a cow, but this wasn't an English assignment. I was just writing my best friend.

I folded the letter, placed it in an envelope, and sealed it, setting it aside to give to Jenny to take to him.

I had the house phone number for Nick, and Jenny had suggested I call Nick's mom. I took several deep breaths and lifted the receiver of Jack and Jenny's house phone. I punched the numbers and listened to the burring of the phone ringing on the other end, working hard not to hang up instead. I had convinced myself that nobody was home and I could leave a message saying hello when Ms. Winslow answered.

"Hello?"

She sounded tired. I guess I couldn't blame her.

"Ms. Winslow?" I said.

"Yes."

"This is Maureen."

"Oh, yes. What can I do for you?" she said. "I'm kind of busy right now."

I wondered if she might still be mad at me for what I'd done. "Oh, sorry. I can call back later."

"No. Since you've called, we might as well find out what it's about."

I took a breath, realizing I wasn't sure why I had called other than Jenny suggested it. Then I remembered what she'd said.

"I didn't mention it when we spoke, so I'm calling to say how sorry I am about your husband. I nearly lost my mom and grandma in the past couple of weeks, and it occurred to me how much losing your husband must have hurt."

I listened to the silence on the other end and

wondered if I'd said something wrong. I waited and was about to speak again when she said, "Thank you." I could hear the emotion in her voice and was sorry I had dredged up her loss.

"I apologize if I've made you sad. I just wanted to tell you how sorry I am."

"No, no. You haven't made me sad, not really. I just think it's so nice of you to call me like this, especially after our conversation before. That's very nice of you."

"Thank you. You see, my mom was in a car accident and now she's doing physical therapy in this place where she's staying, and my grandma had a heart attack and is in the hospital."

"So you're home with your dad?" she asked, obviously not knowing my history, which I didn't want to share. We'd not talked about that at all before.

"No. My dad's gone. I'm staying with some friends of my mom. An attorney in town named Jack Turner and his wife, Jenny. She's the therapist who's seeing Nick.

I heard a quick gasp on the other end of the line. "Her husband's an attorney?"

"Yes, ma'am. He has offices here and in Wharton."

"Tell me," she said. I could hear some slight hesitation in her voice. "Is her husband nice?"

"Yes."

"Is he honest? Do you think he can be trusted?"

I wondered if she was leading up to asking me if he'd gotten "funny" with me.

"Oh, absolutely. He's a really nice man and a

good attorney, too. He doesn't—you know—get too familiar with me or anything like that."

She chuckled and I realized that wasn't what she was asking about.

"Oh, dear. No, I wasn't asking for that reason, though I'm glad to hear he's not like that. I just find I need to consult an attorney about a matter and needed to know if he was a good one, but most importantly, an honest one who could be trusted."

"Oh, yes. He's very honest and he enjoys helping people. He sometimes works for free even."

"Thank you, dear. I will give him a call. Jack Turner?"

"Yes, ma'am."

"Well, this call has been a blessing. You've helped me very much."

I smiled. "I'm glad I could help you. Nick means a lot to me."

"And you mean a lot to him."

I hesitated but then decided it wouldn't hurt to get her on my side in getting Nick to talk to me. "I'm not so sure about that."

"Why not?"

I told her about my visit and how he'd acted.

"Oh, my. I'm sorry. He shouldn't be that way."

"It's okay, really. I wrote him a long letter. I hope it makes him think about talking to me again."

"I'll tell him he should continue being your friend and that he should be nicer to you. He was raised better than that."

"Thanks. But don't be mad with him, okay?"

"I won't. He's going through a lot, and once he gets perspective, I'm sure he'll go back to being himself again."

We chatted for a few more minutes and finally hung up. She thanked me for calling three more times before we disconnected. By the time we hung up, I felt much better about a lot of things, especially my big mistake at school, and I was really happy I helped Ms. Winslow find an attorney. I knew whatever it was, Jack could help.

30

When she'd hung up from talking to Maureen, Holly sat still, gripping her phone as if it might be a lifeline. Maureen's mother trusted this lawyer enough to let her daughter stay with them while she recovered from a car wreck. That was a lot of trust.

She checked the time. She didn't have to pick up Jimmy from school for a while. She couldn't place the call she needed to place here inside the house, nor could she call with Jimmy around. She'd grown paranoid about eavesdroppers, and it was a matter of protection for Jimmy.

Thumbing her phone to open Google, she entered the name of Jack Turner, adding "attorney" to the search. His website popped up at the top of the list. She stepped outside, moving away from the house. Then taking a deep breath to calm herself as well as she could, she entered the number and listened as the phone on the other end rang.

"Shelton and Turner," a woman's voice answered.

At first, Holly froze, unable to speak.

"Hello?" the voice asked.

The thought the woman might hang up pushed Holly from her daze.

"Hi, I'm sorry. I need an attorney." It sounded stupid, even to her.

"Yes, ma'am. How may I help you?"

"Is Mr. Turner taking new clients? I really want to deal with him only. It's probably something he could deal with in a day. Two at the most."

"Certainly. Would you like to schedule an appointment to speak to him?"

"Umm…yes, please." A car drove past, and Holly watched it, aware of the fear and paranoia gripping her as it drove by. Her life was a mess. She needed to get these papers to Mr. Turner. "As soon as possible, please," she added.

"Are you okay?" the person asked, concern evident in her tone.

"Huh?—Yes. It's just that, well, it's urgent I see him as soon as I can. I'd even pay for an after-hours meeting if he's willing."

"Ma'am, you sound frightened. Are you okay?"

"Sorry. Yes. I'm fine."

After a brief pause, the woman asked, "Could I get your name?"

"Holly Winslow."

"And your phone number?"

Holly answered the half-dozen questions to provide a means of contact. Then the woman said, "Hold on, Ms. Winslow. I'll connect you with Mr. Turner's legal secretary. She'll handle setting up the appointment."

"Thank you," Holly said as she was placed on hold.

A moment later, someone else was on the line.

"This is Jasmine Greely, Mr. Turner's secretary. I understand you wish to make an appointment with Mr. Turner?"

"Yes."

"And your name?"

"Holly Winslow."

"Hello, Ms. Winslow. May I ask what this is in regards to?"

Holly froze. She wasn't prepared to talk to anyone else about this, especially not over her cell. "I'd rather talk to Mr. Turner only about this. It's a very private matter."

A brief pause was followed by Ms. Greely saying, "That's fine. I just want to make sure it's something Mr. Turner will handle. Some people call about filing a lawsuit, but Mr. Turner is strictly a criminal defense attorney. Are you accused of a crime?"

"I'm not filing a lawsuit or anything like that. I just need to speak with Mr. Turner, and only Mr. Turner about this." She felt the tears welling. "Ms. Greely, I might be in danger. I need to speak to Mr. Turner as soon as humanly possible. I'll pay anything for just ten minutes of his time. Please."

The sound of desperation must have worked.

"Is this the Ms. Winslow whose husband was murdered a few weeks ago?"

"Yes."

"Hang on, Ms. Winslow. I'm going to connect you to him."

Holly was again put on hold before she could say anything. A moment later, Jack Turner was on the phone.

"Ms. Winslow? This is Jack Turner. How may I help you?"

Holly watched another car drive by and felt

herself instinctively clutch her purse.

She gathered her thoughts and cleared her throat before speaking.

"Mr. Turner, it turns out my son is friends with the young girl staying at your house. Something happened today that requires I find an attorney, and then she called me to tell me how sorry she was that my husband had died and mentioned she was staying with you. I saw it as a sign of sorts since I had only today found out I needed an attorney."

She was rambling and knew it, recognizing the panic that threatened to seize her.

"I'm sorry," she continued. "I know that has nothing to do with anything really. I'm just so scared. I need to meet with you, face-to-face."

"My office closes at five. Can you be here then? I'm in my Denton office today."

Relief washed over her in sudden waves that made her legs feel weak.

"Can I bring my son Jimmy? He'll need to wait outside your office, though. I don't want him in the room with us."

"Certainly. I'll see you at five."

"Thank you! How much will this cost?"

"We'll call it an initial interview. No charge for this meeting."

"Thank you so much for this, Mr. Turner."

When Holly had disconnected, she looked up the address for Jack Turner's Denton office on his website. She admired his photo for a moment, which showed a handsome man somewhere in his mid-to-late fifties and a beautiful dog seated beside him, and she wondered how current the picture was.

When she picked Jimmy up at school, they drove to the local library. It was the safest place she could think of to wait until her meeting with Mr. Turner. Jimmy, always enthusiastic about going to the library, quickly found several books to begin reading. She sat nearby as he read, watching the clock and clutching her purse, as if every patron might try to snatch it.

When it was time to drive to Mr. Turner's office, she gathered Jimmy and the books he wanted to check out, and they drove the three miles to his office.

Entering, she was directed through some doors, where she was greeted by Ms. Greely.

"Good afternoon, Ms. Winslow," she said, smiling. "Mr. Turner will be with you in a moment." Turning to Jimmy, she said, "Would you like something to drink, a Coke or something, or a snack?"

Jimmy looked at his mom to get silent permission. When she nodded, he said, "A Coke, please. What kinds of snacks do you have?"

Ms. Greely named several popular snacks, and Jimmy chose a less healthy individual pack of chocolate chip cookies.

Ms. Greely asked Holly, "Anything for you? Coffee maybe?"

"No, thank you," Holly said.

As Ms. Greely arrived back with Jimmy's snack and drink, her phone buzzed. Answering, she said, "Okay" and hung up.

"He'll see you now, Ms. Winslow." The woman indicated a door opposite the one that led to the reception area.

The door opened before Holly got to it, and a smiling Jack Turner stood there, extending his hand as she entered. She took it and was led into his spacious office.

As he sat next to her rather than behind the massive desk, he said, "Now, what can I do for you?"

She gathered her thoughts for the thousandth time before answering.

"Mr. Turner, when my husband died, I had no idea why he was killed other than he knew something that would be bad for his former employer. We were forced to move from our home in California and go into hiding. My late husband suspected they had found us in Grand Rapids, and we were forced to move again. That's what led us here."

She watched as Jack Turner sat quietly, listening to her story without interruption.

"Anyway, he never explained exactly what he knew. He's an accountant, so I figured it had something to do with finances. He never even told me that much. I just knew, you know?" She paused.

"So after he was killed, I received our next bank statement. That was yesterday. When I opened it, I found he had a safe-deposit box. We'd never had one before, at least not that I ever knew, and I wondered what might be in this one."

"Where is the safe-deposit box?"

"At Florida National Bank here in town."

He nodded. "Okay. Go ahead."

"So, I went searching for the key to the box. I

knew I'd have to have it to see its contents if I didn't want to wait until the estate had been dealt with. I found it and went to the bank today."

Reaching into her large purse, she withdrew a stack of documents with a hand-written document on top of the stack. She handed Jack the hand-written letter from Brad first, feeling it would explain why she was here.

When he'd finished, he said, "I suppose I'm the attorney you've chosen for this task."

"Are you willing to do it?"

"Of course."

She handed him the stack of financial documents and said, "I'm not sure what is in here that might incriminate Brad's boss back in California. Do you know someone you can trust?"

Jack nodded while glancing over the papers. "Absolutely." After going through the first ten or so, he said, "I'm not an accountant, but apparently, your husband felt a good one could look at these and figure out what was going on, at least to the extent of justifying a search warrant."

"Is your friend a cop?"

"Not a local one. He's with the Florida Department of Law Enforcement, the FDLE. He will pass these on to the FBI."

"It has to be someone he trusts completely. You read my late husband's letter."

"You don't have to worry about that." Lifting the phone receiver, he said, "Are you wanting me to go ahead with this?"

"Yes. How much will it cost me?"

"Only the time it took to come here, Ms.

Winslow. Doing this is my public duty."

He punched a few numbers into the phone and said, "Jaz? Could you see if you can get Tom on the line? I need him to deliver some documents first thing in the morning. And come in my office for a second. I have an emergency copying session that needs to be done before you leave."

He hung up and said, "I'll handle it from here."

Holly began to cry from relief. "I'm so sorry I had to get everyone to work late tonight."

"We're sorry you lost your husband only because he was a good man."

When Jaz entered the office, he handed the documents to her. "I need four copies of each of these, collated. Lock them all with the originals in the safe when you're done."

"Certainly, Jack," the woman said. Smiling, she placed a soothing hand on Holly's shoulder. "Don't worry. Your problem belongs to us now."

That night, Holly did her best to sleep, but it took a long time to get everything out of her head

Her final thought before drifting off was, "Now, if I could only do something about Nick."

31

When I handed Jenny my letter to Nick for her to deliver to him, she asked if she could read it. I'd already sealed it in an envelope, but she said it would really be best if she read it first. I suspected she was making sure I wasn't saying anything that might upset Nick, and I realized that I didn't know enough about psychology to know I hadn't done that, so I let her open it and read it.

When she'd finished, she looked at me, smiling. "I think this is just what he needs to hear."

"I don't want him to be upset or anything."

"He might be, but for the right reasons. He should have talked to you, and while explainable, his reaction to your visit was rude."

"If he wants to see me again, will you take me?"

"Sure."

"Jenny?"

"Yes?"

"Will you also take me to see my grandmother and my mom one day this week?"

"Of course. How does tomorrow sound?"

"That would be great!"

I sealed the letter in a fresh envelope, and Jenny took it.

The next day, Jenny came home and we went

to visit my grandmother first since the care facility where she was staying was on the way to the rehab center.

When I entered her room, she looked at me and smiled, but it wasn't a happy smile. Had she been given bad news? I felt panic rising again and pushed it back down.

"Hi, Grandma," I said, trying my best to be cheerful.

"I didn't thank you," she said.

"For what?"

"Calling 9-1-1. I guess you saved my life."

"You don't need to thank me for that. What was I supposed to do? Watch you die?"

"I suppose you're right. It just felt like I should thank you."

She was silent for several minutes, and I wondered if she was too tired for me to visit right then.

"If you want me to go and let you rest, I can."

"No. I'm just thinking about what I need to say to you." She paused again and added, "What I need to tell you."

This must have been the reason for the not-so-happy smile. She had been thinking about something she needed to tell me that wouldn't be easy for her and probably not for me either.

She took a deep breath and smoothed the bed covers. Even at my age I knew she was stalling, waiting for the right words to come to her. But sometimes there are no right words, just the ones we have to say whether we want to or not.

"A part of me has always hated your mother."

It was an odd way to start whatever she wanted to say. Her words left me feeling cold, as if a draft of winter air had run up my spine. She seemed to be waiting for me to respond, but I wasn't sure how to do that. I mean, what do you say to your grandmother when she tells you "a part" of her always hated your mom? So instead of saying anything that meant something, I just said, "Oh."

"Yes. I wanted to tell you about this and see if it will help our own relationship. You see, because a part of me has hated her, I have sort of passed that on to resenting you sometimes."

I didn't want to hear this, but I knew I had to anyway. I did my best to keep from crying, at least until I was out of that room. I felt my eyes tear up, but I managed to hold it in for the time being.

"I don't say that to hurt you," she said.

"Then why did you say it?" I asked and waited to be crushed.

"The truth is that there comes a point in our lives that we need to explain ourselves, even if those we want to explain to don't understand. The hope is that one day you will, and you'll be able to forgive me."

I wasn't sure I could do that. My grandmother was admitting she resented me, maybe hated me. How does someone forgive their grandmother for that?

I felt anger rising in me and held it back. It wouldn't help to start yelling at her. I'd probably be dragged from the room if I did. I suddenly wished Jenny was there, but she'd excused herself when we arrived at Grandma's room. Did she know this conversation would be happening?

I waited a second before saying, "You mentioned explaining yourself. So explain."

"The truth is I'm not a good person sometimes. I have problems with jealousy."

"Does this have to do with how my mom got pregnant with me?"

She looked at the covers over her chest and nodded quickly as if she didn't want to admit it.

"So your ex-husband, my mom's stepfather, raped her. Seems to me you'd appreciate knowing what an—" I almost said a bad word but stopped myself in time. "What a jerk he was."

"It was more than that." I noticed a tear running down Grandma's cheek. That she was crying shocked me. I'd only seen her tear up once before.

"What do you mean?"

"I knew he was attracted to your mother from early on, but I ignored it, figuring he wouldn't do anything about it, mostly due to her age. It turned out he waited until she was twenty before raping her. Besides, she hated him."

She reached for a tissue and dabbed her eyes. "But part of her liked the attention he gave her, despite all that. I hated her for that." After a moment, she added, "And a lot of other things. Her running away with that boy hurt me deeply. Part of me didn't really care that she killed him, but I was scared beyond belief that she would end up in prison. She would have if not for Jack Turner."

"Do you think she killed him on purpose?" I asked, finally wanting to know the answer.

"I don't know. I think she certainly wanted to

and just acted—or reacted—when the time came. I don't really care if it was on purpose. When she got home, she moved out within a few months to go live with Mrs. Dawson after we had an argument."

"What was the argument about?"

"I don't remember. Isn't that funny? It was life-changing for all of us, but I don't remember what it was about. I guess it shows how silly such arguments can be."

"So then, you hated my mom because she moved out?"

"And because my husband was more interested in her than in me. That's a difficult thing to realize and deal with." She tried to look at me but immediately dropped her eyes. "It can make a woman feel worthless."

"If Mom didn't like him, why do you hate her for that? It wasn't her fault he was like that."

"That didn't matter. He still wanted her more than he wanted me, so I was jealous."

"And you hate me because I came from that sick desire he had?"

"I resented you. I think hate is too strong a word." She looked at me this time, holding my gaze despite both of us wanting to look away. "I'm telling you this so you'll understand why our relationship has been difficult and—" She took a shuddering breath. "And to tell you that I don't resent you anymore." She paused. "I love you."

She looked down at the covers again and continued. "I might not have long left on this world, and I want whatever time I have left to be happier." She looked back into my eyes. "For all of us, your mother included."

"Does she know you've hated her?"

"It's hard to put into words. I both hated her and loved her at the same time. I never told her I hated her, but I'm sure she knows ours was a love/hate relationship, just as you've known my feelings for you down deep inside."

She was right, of course. I had known all along that she didn't like me very much. I just hadn't known why.

"You know, I was also jealous of the relationship your mother had with Mrs. Dawson, but even though I was jealous of the woman, she did teach me something valuable that I'm only now figuring out was true."

"What's that?"

"If you don't accept responsibility for the problems in your life, they will always be problems. They will haunt you."

My look of not quite understanding prompted her to explain.

"You see, when people blame others for the situations in their lives, they always have a reason not to deal with the situation. They can always disavow any responsibility for whatever is wrong. 'I'm poor because I was born into poverty.' Or 'I can't get ahead because my boss won't give me a promotion.' It's just a basket of excuses. Your lot in life is what you make it."

"Some people have mental illnesses that keep them from being happy."

"That's different. I'm talking about people who have the ability to do something about their lives."

I thought about what she meant. "I guess you did hear that from Mrs. Dawson. That sounds like what Mom calls a Dawsonism," I said.

"It wasn't until much later that I realized how wise the woman was, but by then, we didn't speak to each other. I wouldn't speak to her because I was jealous of her relationship with my daughter. She wouldn't speak to me because I refused to speak to her." She sighed. "Just another of life's regrets."

Then she caught my gaze again. "I don't want our relationship to become another regret in my life. Or yours. I think we've all suffered mountains of regret."

We talked until Jenny came back. I could tell from the surprise on her face at seeing that we'd both been crying that she had no idea what we would be talking about when she dropped me off.

After we left the elder care facility and were driving to the rehab center where my mom was getting physical therapy, I realized that Grandma must be coming face-to-face with death and had realized she needed to talk to me, though it would probably be several years before she died. I hoped she would talk to Mom later as well. I wasn't sure if I should tell Mom what we'd talked about, so I didn't until months later.

My visit with Mom was good, though she could tell something was bothering me. Instead of telling her about my conversation with Grandma, I told her I was worried about Nick and whether he would talk to me again. That seemed to satisfy Mom, and we chatted until Jenny stopped by to get me.

It was nice of Jenny to give me alone time with

my grandmother and my mom. I don't know where she went, but I figured she had gone for some coffee or something.

That night after I went to bed, I decided to write down what had happened that day with my grandma and my mom. I had brought my journal with me and pulled it out to begin writing while it was still fresh in my mind.

I'm glad I did that, especially now. It helps me remember how life went at the time, which wasn't easy at all. In fact, it could be more than painful.

32

Nick sat staring at the still unopened envelope. A small heart formed the dot of the "i" in Nick. It was typical of Maureen to do that. As he sat holding the envelope, he dreaded opening it. Despite the heart, he figured she was going to tell him how angry she was and how she never wanted to see or speak to him again. He knew even as he had done it how badly he'd treated her, but he couldn't explain why he'd been so mean to her.

Through his sessions, he'd finally realized that she was only trying to help him keep in contact with his friends by creating the email address for him. It was something he could have done himself, but she'd taken it upon herself to do that, neither of them realizing the hidden consequences.

His time with Ms. Turner had taught him that sometimes people make mistakes, sometimes big ones, especially when they're young and don't understand the possible outcome. He'd not even known his dad was running for his life, only that his family didn't want to be found. As Ms. Turner had reminded him, he was only thirteen—old enough to feel grown up while being anything but an adult.

Ms. Turner had left a few minutes ago and had handed him the envelope just before leaving.

"I suppose you will want to read this alone," she'd said. "That's why I've waited until now to give it to you. Consider her words with care and understanding, please."

That last comment led him to believe she'd read the letter already. With another heart drawn over the back flap like some old-timey seal, Nick figured Maureen had let Ms. Turner read it.

Knowing he would need to read it sooner or later since Ms. Turner would probably ask about it when they saw each other in a few days, he opened the envelope by slitting the top edge and taking care not to tear the heart seal.

Pulling the sheet from inside, he opened it, bracing himself for the anger he expected.

As he read, he waited for the other shoe to drop. He kept expecting her to bless him out for the way he treated her—maybe even curse, which wasn't like her—but instead she seemed understanding.

She wasn't angry at all, only sad and hurt. He felt shame wash over him. She hadn't deserved that treatment any more than he had deserved having his father murdered.

Until that moment, he had felt only his mother and brother really cared. Maybe Ms. Turner, but it was her job to help him, or at least try. This letter told him he'd been wrong. Maureen cared. She was a friend in the truest sense.

He was allowed to use the phone at the facility where he was staying. Ms. Turner had given him her cell number, and he wanted to let her know that she should bring Maureen the next time she came. Pulling her business card from a drawer beside his bed, he went to the front desk and asked to use the phone.

"Who you gonna call?" she asked.

"My therapist, Ms. Turner."

She nodded and pointed at the phone on her desk, indicating he could have a seat. "Make it fast, though. If another line rings, I have to answer it."

He dialed Ms. Turner's number and waited while the call went through. When she answered, he said, "Ms. Turner? It's Nick."

"Yes, Nick?" She sounded as if she'd expected his call.

"Would you be able to bring Maureen with you the next time you come? I want to apologize to her."

"Certainly. I can bring her by tomorrow afternoon when she gets home from school if you'd like. There's no need to wait until our next session."

"That would be good."

"Okay. We'll see you tomorrow. And Nick?"

"Yes?"

"I'm glad you're doing the right thing. That's a big step forward."

"Thanks."

After hanging up, he went to his room and thought about his life. Mostly, he thought about his future. The past was the past and he couldn't change that. He missed his dad, but Maureen was right. His father's death was the fault of the people who sent the guy to kill him. He should have had the right to communicate with his friends without worrying that something bad would happen because he had.

As he lay on his bed, he found himself smiling for the first time in a long time. It was only a small

257

smile, but it felt good. Maybe things would be okay after all.

33

I felt anxious waiting for Jenny to come home the day she delivered my letter to Nick. It wasn't until that day that I realized Nick might tell me to buzz off. I'd written it with the hope that he would accept my offer of friendship, but now it occurred to me that he might not. I wasn't sure how I would handle that. Waiting was making me crazy, so I fixed myself a bowl of mint chocolate chip ice cream to take my mind off my worries.

Of course, that only lasted about fifteen minutes. I mean, once the ice cream was gone, what then? Yoga?

I decided to call my mom and talk to her about it, but she was in a rehab session and couldn't talk to me. She answered but told me to call back in a half hour.

I set a kitchen timer for thirty minutes and waited, doing my best to think of other things, which didn't work, of course. Mom would have said I was like a dog with a bone, and I suppose she was right. I couldn't leave it alone, and all the possible bad outcomes of my letter kept rolling around in my head.

Finally, the timer went off, and I called Mom again. She sounded out of breath, so now I was worried about her.

"What are they doing? Making you run miles?"

"No, honey. The exercises can be strenuous though. They wear me out sometimes."

I shifted gears back to the problem that had been gnawing at me, and I realized that maybe I was the bone in the analogy my mom sometimes used.

I told her about the letter I wrote Nick without mentioning my role in his situation and how Jenny was delivering it today, and I was nervous about it.

"Sweetheart, I understand you're worried he might not want to be your friend, but I have a question. If he tells Jenny he never wants to see you again, what can you do about it?"

"I could try calling him."

"Do you think that would change anything? Do you believe he'll think, 'Oh, well, she called me, so I guess I should change my mind'?"

That she was right bothered me. "No."

"Honey, we can't make people like us. They either do or they don't. My guess is he might not respond well now, but he could in the future after he thinks about it. He's in a rough place right now in his life. He just lost his father, and he's angry at the world. And the world includes you."

"But he was my best friend!"

"And he may end up your best friend again. Give it time, but realize you can't force him to do anything, especially where it concerns accepting your friendship."

Heaving a deep sigh, I said, "Okay."

"Besides, you don't have his answer yet. It's entirely possible you're worrying over nothing. Tell you what, ask Jenny about grandfather clocks, even if she has good news for you."

"Grandfather clocks?" What did they have to do with anything?

"Yes."

"What will she tell me about grandfather clocks that have anything to do with this?"

"Just ask her."

"Can't you tell me?"

"No. It's her story. Just ask. It's something you need to hear, and she will love to tell you about it."

She changed the subject, asking me about school and how I was doing. There wasn't much to tell. I was doing fine, though math was a killer and I was struggling to make a C.

"Stick with it. Your brain will catch up."

I thought that was a weird answer, but I didn't argue the point.

We chatted about her rehab a bit until I heard Jenny drive up.

"She's here," I said, suddenly excited and scared at the same time. "I'll talk to you later."

"Be sure to let me know what Nick said. You can just text me on Jenny's phone."

"Okay."

I felt the tension drain out of me when I saw Jenny. She was smiling.

"Did you give him my letter?" I asked before realizing that was a stupid question.

"Of course. I left it with him, figuring he wouldn't want to read it right there in front of me. On my drive home, he called. He wants me to bring you to see him again."

"Do you think he really wants to talk to me, or

261

does he want to bless me out?"

"I'm sure he just wants to talk to you. I think he already 'blessed you out,' as you say."

"When can I go?"

"How does tomorrow after school sound?"

"Great!" Then I remembered my mom wanted me to text her. "Can I borrow your phone? I called Mom and talked to her about this, and she wanted me to text her on your phone what Nick's answer was."

"Sure," she said and fished her phone out of her purse.

I found Mom in the contacts and sent her the text that Nick wanted to see me tomorrow. When her reply came back, it said, "That's wonderful. Now, ask Jenny about grandfather clocks, and you'll understand why I asked you to do that."

As Jenny started pulling things from the refrigerator to prepare dinner, I handed her phone back to her and said, "Mom wants me to ask you about grandfather clocks for some reason."

Jenny chuckled and said, "So, you were worried about what you'd do if Nick didn't want to see you, huh?"

I nodded, wondering again what a clock had to do with my worrying about what Nick would do. It was obvious it did, given how Jenny immediately figured out why Mom had told me to ask about them.

Grinning at me, she said, "Once upon a time, there were these two old ladies who lived together in a big house. One of the ladies found the other lady sitting next to a big grandfather clock one day, crying. 'Why are you crying?' the first lady asked. 'What if one of my grandchildren had been playing in here one day and knocked that huge clock over, making it fall over and kill him?' the woman said."

Jenny looked at me to see if I got the message. I was puzzled for a moment, but then it hit me. "She was worried about something that had never happened and never would."

Jenny winked at me. "Smart girl."

"But the thing with Nick saying he never wanted to see me again was possible."

"Yes, but it wasn't worth worrying about since you had no control over it. I'm not saying I don't do the same thing sometimes, but the truth is we worry about a lot of things that will never happen. Sometimes, we just need to wait for the outcome, especially if we have no power to change it."

She was right, of course. I had worked myself up over what turned out to be nothing. Nick had accepted my wish to see him again and be his friend. I'd worried so much about it, I'd eaten a huge bowl of ice cream.

I looked over to see Jenny was fixing some leftover pot roast from two nights before.

"I'm not sure how much I'll eat tonight."

"Oh? Are you not feeling well?"

"No, I feel fine, but I worried so much over the letter that I ate a big bowl of ice cream."

Jenny laughed. "Ice cream doesn't last that long. I'm sure you'll be hungry by dinner time."

The next day, I thought about going to see Nick so much I was distracted from what was going on in my classes. Ms. Henderson called on me in class, and I didn't even hear her. The other kids laughed as I sat deep in thought until she called on me a second time.

When I got home, I did my homework. Then Jenny arrived and I bounded out to the car.

We chatted about things as she drove, and I told her about what had happened in English class that day.

"Hopefully, you won't be so distracted after today," she said.

When we arrived, we met with Nick. He was more pleasant than he was the last time, and I could see he felt sorry for how he'd behaved before.

"I'll leave the two of you to talk," Jenny said after a few minutes and left to have a cup of coffee or something.

We sat in awkward silence for a moment, and I decided to be the one to break the ice.

"I'm really glad you wanted to see me."

"Yeah. I'm sorry for how I acted. You didn't deserve that."

"I understand. I wasn't happy, but I understood why you felt that way. I can see how you feel I had a hand in your father's death."

"No. You were right. It wasn't your fault or even mine. They probably would have found us some other way. My mom told me that's why we moved from Grand Rapids. My dad suspected they'd found us there, and I didn't email anyone. I guess it's harder to disappear than I thought."

"Nick?"

"Yeah?"

"Why did you try to kill yourself?"

He looked at his knees and seemed to think for a moment, but in the end, he just shrugged. "I don't know. I was just too sad to live, I guess. I heard a lot of people kill themselves because they're in pain that they don't want to deal with anymore."

"But there's always a better way. Killing yourself might put you out of misery, but it leaves everyone else having to deal with that."

"Yeah. I know that now. I guess I didn't think about it before."

"So be honest. Are you planning to do it again?"

"No. And that's the truth. I don't want to die anymore." He thought for a moment. "I want to see the people who killed my dad go to prison. If I died, I wouldn't be able to see that."

"That could take years."

"Then that's what it'll take."

"Your mom probably won't let you go to the trial."

"That's okay. The trial doesn't matter, only the verdict. I just want them to pay for what they did. And besides, if they're behind bars, they won't come after my mom." He considered this. "Or me and Jimmy."

Looking at me, he said, "I want to talk about something else now."

"Okay, like what?"

"Are people talking about me at school?"

"They were at first, but not anymore. My mom used to say the news is like the weather. Wait a day and it will change. You were big news at first, but it's blown over. Kids might look at you when you come back, but after a couple of days, they'll just be back to their normal selves."

"I'm not looking forward to returning to school, but I guess I'll have to one day soon."

"I don't blame you. Mia misses you, though," I said, changing the subject.

"That's nice," he said, obviously not really caring.

"Should I tell her, or will you?"

"Tell her what?"

"That you don't like her anymore, at least not like a girlfriend."

"I should tell her, but you can drop the hint to make it less painful when I do."

"Do you know when you'll be coming back to school?"

"No, but it should be soon. Ms. Turner said deciding to see you like this would help get me out of here."

"How?"

"I don't know, but she said it was a huge step in my recovery. I hope I can come home by this weekend and start back with my normal life."

"That would be good."

We kept talking until Jenny came back. When I asked why she'd come back so soon, she said we'd been talking for over an hour. Both of us were surprised and we both laughed. His laughter, which I'd not heard in what felt like forever, sounded like a beautiful song I'd forgotten.

As we drove home, I told Jenny about what Nick had said about seeing me was a huge step in his recovery and asked why that was.

"Because it shows he's ready to move on and accept his mistakes."

"Did you tell him that before he saw me?"

"No. I couldn't influence his thinking like that. If I'd said anything, he might have said he'd see you just to help him move back home. His reasons for seeing you had to be, well, pure. He had to want to see you because he wanted to see you, not because it would suggest he was getting much better."

"Is he much better?"

"Yes. In fact, I'm starting the paperwork to have him released tomorrow. He doesn't want to kill himself anymore."

"I knew that because he told me."

"He told me that too, but I needed more than his word. People are good at fooling others sometimes. I needed concrete evidence that he was no longer a danger to himself. To be honest, the other day when he was not pleasant to you, I wondered how long it would take for him to move on. I think you helped him a lot."

It felt good to think I had done something good for someone else, especially a friend.

When we arrived home, I went inside and began a letter to Nick. This one was about normal stuff. I didn't mention his dad once. Mostly, I talked about Bluebelle and how sweet a dog she was and how funny she could be, like sometimes she would sit very still, not moving her head at all. It reminded me of a pelican sitting and looking at the water.

That Monday, Nick returned to school. The day went how I had figured it would. Lots of kids stared at him, but only a few said anything to him. Most of those were kids welcoming him back. I think even the kids who stared without saying anything were happy he hadn't succeeded. Still, they saw him differently now.

Not all of the kids were nice about it, though. I finally grew fed-up with one kid staring and pointing while laughing with his friends. I knew whatever he was saying wasn't nice. I looked at him until he saw me noticing him and said, "What's wrong with you? He's been through a lot more than you have! Leave him alone!"

Nick reached out and touched my arm. "It's okay. Like you said, they'll move on to something else in another few days."

I was glad he was adjusting so well. Mia was broken-hearted about him not wanting to be her boyfriend anymore, but she managed to find a new one in a couple of days. It wasn't as if there weren't a dozen guys lined up to be her boyfriend.

Now, it was mostly Cameron and me hanging out with Nick, but that felt more comfortable. Cameron was an understanding person and was thrilled to see Nick again. Ms. Henderson was so happy he was back, I thought she was going to give him a welcome back to school party. She didn't though, but it would have been nice if she had. I mean, who doesn't prefer a party to doing schoolwork?

34

A month after Nick returned to school, Jack was on the phone with Tom discussing an investigation Tom was conducting for him when the crucial email arrived. It was from his friend with the FDLE that he'd given the documents from Holly Winslow to. His computer screen was open to his email, and he saw the new one pop up at the top of his inbox. He noticed the subject line: "You found the next Madoff/Enron."

"Tom, I'll have to call you back. Something just came up."

"Sure thing," Tom said. "Just let me know where you want me to go with this."

Hanging up, Jack opened the email. All it said was, "Call me ASAP."

Looking up the number in his phone, Jack dialed it on his office phone, which was checked weekly for bugs, along with his office. Privacy was sacrosanct for Jack where his clients were concerned, and he didn't always trust others to respect that privacy.

When John Bourret, his friend, answered, he said, "Jack, thanks for calling back."

"So what's up? Madoff? Enron? You mean it's that big?"

"Maybe bigger. I hand-delivered the papers to a friend in the FBI. He just called and told me an

269

indictment would surely come from this. They had their forensic accountant look at it, and he said it's more than enough to get a search warrant for all the company's financial records. Don't say anything because he wasn't supposed to tell me, but it's going to be big, like national news. They managed to flip another accountant."

"John, a man was murdered over this."

"So that's what this is about. All you had time to tell me when we spoke on the phone before was someone you trusted had brought you the documents, and you'd promised to pass them on to me. Can you elaborate now?"

"The victim was an accountant for the firm in question. He'd gone into hiding, moving twice in the span of a few months, but he was found somehow. He opened his door one night and was shot dead. An obvious hit. The woman who brought me the papers is his widow. She'd found the papers in a safe-deposit box she'd been unaware of. I know local murders don't cross your radar, but it's part of this."

"Wow. This goes deep."

"Yeah."

"I'll be sure to pass that on to my friend in the FBI. Why didn't you say something when we spoke after Tom delivered the papers?"

"I didn't want to muddy the waters. I felt that if there was nothing, we could move on, and I didn't want a murder clouding the initial investigation. Besides, financial crimes have a statute of limitations, though those limitations were far from running out. Murder has no such limitation. The limitation the law provides for financial crimes might make the FBI move faster on this, and they could focus on that one crime, rather than two or even more. It can take years to complete an investigation of this sort. I suppose this one will take at least that long."

"My friend said it was pretty clear from the paperwork that a scheme was in place to cheat investors out of billions of dollars."

"Billions? With a B?"

"Yes. Whoever this accountant was that was killed knew what to keep. I imagine there are two sets of books. I'm left wondering how this guy was allowed to see the illegal transactions."

"I don't know, but he was. Maybe he was suspicious and managed to get ahold of them without his employer knowing. I do know he went to his boss about this, and it was after that he decided he needed to disappear."

"Well, thanks for this. It's going to be big."

They chatted for a few more minutes before disconnecting the call. Then Jack dialed Holly Winslow.

After she answered, he said, "Hi, Holly. This is Jack. I need you to come to my office as soon as possible. There's been a development that you need to hear, and I don't want to discuss it over the phone."

"Can I come now?"

"Yes. I can push anything that comes up until later."

When she arrived, she was shown immediately into Jack's office.

"We've hit the jackpot," he said.

"What do you mean?"

Jack went on to explain the depth of the criminal enterprise her husband had uncovered. "I was told it was at least as big of a financial scandal as the Bernie Madoff or Enron scandals."

"Oh, my Lord. No wonder they wanted to kill him," she said.

"Did he ever tell you how he came to have those documents?"

"No. He said he didn't want me to know much of anything for my own safety."

"I hope the FBI can find the original files. If not, this might not go very far."

"Why would they keep records of illegal transactions?"

"Because it's always about the money. Criminals at this scale need to know where the money is going and where it's coming from. The difference is that those books are never shown to the IRS or any other government entity."

"How would Brad have access to stuff like that if they didn't want it seen?"

"I don't know. He probably wasn't supposed to see anything and stumbled on it. That would be my guess."

"Do you think they'll find the original documents? The proof of their scheme, whatever it was?"

"That's the question of the hour, but they can be very thorough and meticulous in their searches. They likely will, or maybe already have since they managed to get one of the firm's accountants to flip, which is a major bonus."

"If they don't find the proof, I might have to go into hiding and keep running from them the rest of my life."

"Hopefully, that won't become necessary."

She stared at him. "How much would it cost to hire someone to be a sort of bodyguard?"

The fear in her eyes was nearly palpable as Jack looked back at her.

"I have an old friend in the police department. Detective Sergeant Bob Ebert. I'll have him make sure a cruiser comes by your house to check on things several times a day, with increased watch overnight. Would that make you feel better?"

Her small smile quivered from her shattered nerves.

When Holly had left, he called the Denton Police Department and asked to speak to Bob. He wasn't there, but the person answering said he would get word to him to call as soon as he could.

Ten minutes later, he was talking to what was one of several childhood enemies he'd dealt with growing up. Like Tom, Bob had become a friend, though not as close a friend as Tom had.

When Jack had explained the situation, Bob said he would make sure a car drove by the Winslow home every couple of hours at the very least, saying the last thing he needed was to deal with the murder of Brad Winslow's entire family.

Hanging up, Jack moved on to other work. The wheels of justice had begun their slow crawl.

35

Nick was becoming more like himself each day. He and Cameron and I would meet in our usual spot in the cafeteria and talk and even laugh. Mia had found another group to hang out with. I would see her looking at us sometimes, and understood the expression, "if looks could kill." I'd heard from more than one person that she thought I had stolen Nick from her. Nothing could be further from the truth, though. I still didn't like him like that. I didn't like any boy like that, in fact.

Mia had asked to switch seats with a boy in science class. The new boy at our table, Eddie, was nice but also not anyone I saw as boyfriend material. I just thought he was funny. He could make funny faces and waggle his eyebrows in ways that made us laugh.

We were working on an experiment for class when Mr. Lance stuck his head in the door. He glanced around and made eye contact with me. I felt my mouth dry up, wondering why he was looking at me out of everyone in the room.

Mr. Clay, my science teacher, went to Mr. Lance, and they exchanged a few words. I watched this exchange, having lost all interest in what we'd been working on. Something was going on that involved me, or at least I thought it did. When Mr. Clay turned and looked at me, I was sure of it.

"Maureen?" he said, as if I weren't looking right at him. "Mr. Lance needs you to go with him."

Wondering what I'd done wrong, I stood and walked to the door where the two men stood. I was considering every possible reason for me to be in trouble but couldn't think of one. Had someone implicated me in something?

Then I thought of it. Mia. She had told some kind of lie to get me in trouble. That had to be it.

But when I looked up at Mr. Lance and Mr. Clay, neither seemed angry as though disappointed in me for doing whatever it was I'd been accused of. They looked sad. They looked like they couldn't think of the right words to tell me something they knew would hurt me. Something bad had happened. Something really dreadful. Awful. Heartbreaking. Devastating. As these words zipped through my thoughts, I discarded each as not bad enough.

"You need to come with me," Mr. Lance said.

We walked in silence to the office. It all felt so surreal that I wondered if this was a nightmare and I would wake up soon. I prayed I would.

As I entered the main office, I was met with more sad looks from the secretaries. Nobody said anything.

I was escorted back to Mr. Lance's office, and was surprised to see Jenny sitting there. She'd been crying.

I was suddenly aware someone had died, and the crazy thought occurred to me that it was Bluebelle, but nobody would be getting me out of class for that.

My mind was spinning in a thousand

275

directions, seemingly unable to land on one thought. Then I asked the dreaded question. "Is it Mom?"

Jenny shook her head and sniffed, dabbing at her eyes. "No, honey. It's your grandmother. She had another heart attack this morning. She's gone."

I heard myself gasp. I felt as though my mind and my body were disconnected, as if I were standing beside myself, not really a part of my body.

How could that be? Jenny had taken me back to visit her yesterday after school. We'd talked and laughed, and Grandma had told me she loves me at least ten times, and I had told her the same. We were going to be friends now. We were going to get along like we never had before. She'd forgiven me for things I didn't need forgiveness for, but her heart had needed. Things were going to be better. She was going to come home soon and take care of me until the doctors released Mom from rehab. Grandma was...dead?

I don't remember much after that, at least for the next little while. All I could do was cry and sob. The thought we would never have the relationship we both wanted and deserved kept hitting me like body blows from a boxer. That thought would punch me, and sobs would slam my body once again. I was sad that she'd not been able to move back home after her heart attack. That would have given us more time together.

The first place Jenny took me when we left school was to see Mom. She was crying when we arrived. This caused a fresh fountain of tears from me, and I wondered if I would get dehydrated from shedding all the tears.

When our tears finally dried up and we were able to talk, Mom said she would need to handle the arrangements, which was like trying to find the words to say something. There was no easy way to do it. It simply had to be done. Life sometimes became a series of events people needed to get past so they could move on.

"I can help you with the arrangements," Jenny said. "Did she want to be cremated or buried?"

"She wanted to be cremated and have her ashes scattered in the Gulf."

This surprised me. I had no idea Grandma had said anything about what should happen when she died.

"Is Atkins Funeral Home okay for handling it?" Jenny asked.

"Yes, that would be fine."

Jenny excused herself for a moment, and Mom and I talked. I hadn't told her about my conversation with Grandma when she'd said she resented me, so I did, saying how it changed our relationship. I left out how Grandma said part of her had hated Mom, but Mom told me that Grandma had phoned her recently and apologized to her as well.

Jenny came back and said she'd called the facility where Grandma was and told them we wanted the body sent to Atkins.

"I think you should call Atkins and make the preliminary arrangements," Jenny said.

Mom looked up the number for Atkins Funeral Home and called. They spoke for about fifteen minutes while Jenny and I sat there and listened to Mom's end of the conversation.

When she'd hung up, Mom said, "They'll cremate her, and we can have a service there." We'd heard her tell them we didn't need a fancy urn since we would be scattering her ashes in the Gulf of Mexico. She told us that they had an inexpensive one for our needs.

"There's some paperwork I have to fill out and sign, of course. They need it filled out as soon as possible. They really can't do anything from just my phone call but accept the body."

"Certainly," Jenny said. "We can go there and bring the paperwork back to you. I can wait while you complete it and take it directly back to them."

"No, I think I want to get out of this place, and this is a perfect excuse."

"Are you sure?" Jenny asked.

"Absolutely."

Jenny went to make arrangements for Mom to be able to leave for a few hours, and Mom and I continued talking about Grandma.

"I was so mean to her as a teenager," Mom said. "I told her I regret how I treated her. She deserved better."

A sudden question occurred to me. "Mom?"

"Yes?"

"What did y'all argue about that made you move out and live with Mrs. Dawson?"

She thought for a moment before sighing. "I don't remember."

It seemed strange to me that neither Mom nor Grandma could recall what had to be a huge fight. It had changed everyone's life. This was no minor spat. It was life-altering.

"Grandma couldn't remember either," I said. "You'd think if it was that important, you'd remember."

"Then I guess it wasn't that important," Mom said. "We just thought it was at the time." Mom looked wistful for a moment, and I changed the subject.

"Can we get a dog when you get home?"

She smiled at me without saying anything. Finally, she said, "We'll see." It was the classic avoidance answer, and under the circumstances, I didn't push it.

Jenny came back, and we loaded Mom into her car for the drive to Atkins Funeral Home. When we arrived, we helped Mom into their office, and she filled out the paperwork, which included details for Grandma's memorial service at Atkins in the chapel they used for such things.

After returning her to the rehab center, Jenny took me home. I played with Bluebelle until that evening, had dinner, and went to bed. I thought I would lie awake for hours, but I guess the day had exhausted me because I fell asleep within minutes.

A few days later, Jenny, Jack, and I dressed for the memorial service. Jenny had taken me to buy a black dress since I didn't have any. I worried that she was spending money on clothes for me, but she told me not to worry, that my mom had told her she would pay her back.

When we arrived at my house to pick up a

dress for Mom, it felt eerie going inside. I hadn't been there since Grandma's first heart attack, and the place smelled musty, as if it needed a good cleaning and airing out. I felt as though I was walking through some past experience or a dream.

We drove to the rehab center, and Jenny helped Mom into her dress. We were finally headed to the funeral home, and Mom asked me if I wanted to say a few words at the service.

"Who will be there?" I asked.

"Just us and Uncle Ryan and his family."

"They're coming?"

"Of course. She was his mom, too."

I hadn't been told they would be there. He was stationed in Germany, so their flight was a long one.

"When did they get into town?"

"Late last night," Mom said.

"Why didn't you tell me they were coming?"

"I forgot in all the hubbub of arranging Grandma's funeral. Besides, I didn't want to disappoint you if they had to cancel for some reason."

"I wondered if they'd come for the funeral but wasn't sure Uncle Ryan had the time," I said.

"People make time for what's important."

I thought about how true that was. If it was important for someone, they made time for it.

"Do I have to talk?" I asked.

"No, not if you don't want to. I just wanted to offer you the opportunity."

I sat in thought as we rode. I thought it was sad that the only people who would be at Grandma's funeral were her two kids, their kids, and Jack and

Jenny. No other friends. Just family and two people who'd known Grandma for years.

It made me hope my own funeral, whenever it was, would be better attended. That Grandma hadn't made a lot of friends hit me, and I started crying again.

Mom put an arm around me and pulled me to her.

As we pulled up, I said, "I'll say something at the service."

Mom asked, "Are you sure? I don't want you to feel obligated. I wanted to make sure you could if you wanted to. I'd hate it if you wanted to say something, but didn't feel okay with doing that."

"No, I'm sure," I said. I already knew what I would talk about.

A man from the funeral home stepped forward when everyone was ready to begin and welcomed us as we "celebrated the life of Lorraine Shaw Regent." He read some information about her life that Mom must have supplied before asking if anyone wanted to say a few words. Mom glanced down at me and I stood up, walking to the podium at the front. The urn was resting on a pedestal in front of the podium. A large picture of Grandma stood on a sort of easel behind where I now stood looking at my mom, my uncle, his wife and three kids, and the Turners. That I knew the Turners much better than I knew my uncle and his family was part of what I would talk about. It wasn't going to be a cheerful sendoff kind of talk. It would be off-the-cuff and sad, but I would end with more positive thoughts. At least I hoped they were. I wasn't crying at all. Not yet, at least. Perhaps I was cried out.

I looked at the tiny gathering and said, "On the way here, I thought about how we would be the only people at Grandma's funeral. If she'd chosen to be buried in the cemetery, we'd have to hire pallbearers." I looked down at the urn. "Maybe that's why she chose to be cremated instead."

I looked at my uncle and his family, who were seated to my left. "I was even surprised that you would all be here. Mom told me that people make time for what's important to them, and that's why you came." Uncle Ryan nodded.

"I'm sorry, but why wasn't visiting her when she was alive important?" I glanced over at Mom, who looked shocked that I would say that.

"Maureen, this isn't the time for this."

"No, Mom. It's actually the perfect time. The fact is we're not a close family, no matter how much I wish we were." I felt my chest tighten and took a breath to ease the pressure.

"People never say they love each other enough. And I don't mean only the words." I looked over at Uncle Ryan, who was hanging his head, but I knew he was listening. "You know, making more time to visit us would tell us you love us." I took another breath. "I know you do. It's just people never take the time to show they love someone beyond the words to say it."

Looking down at the urn, I said, "Grandma was the same way. She really didn't even say she loved me and really mean it until after her heart attack." I looked out at the others. "We were able to have fun visits after that. After that when I visited, she showed me and told me how much she loved me. She was like a different person." I paused. "She smiled. A lot."

A tear slid down my cheek, and I wiped it away, almost angry I had started to weep.

"Here's the truth. If we love each other, we need to start showing it." I glanced over at Jack and Jenny. Their love for me shone in their eyes like bright candles. I pointed at them. "Jack and Jenny love me. They show me all the time. They don't even have to say it." I looked at my uncle and his family. "I think you should start showing it, too."

Looking at Mom, I said, "And we're no better than Uncle Ryan and his family. I know you're in rehab now, but maybe we could take a trip to Germany and visit them sometime?"

I looked at all of them, Mom, the Turners, Uncle Ryan. I said, "We have to start showing how much we care. Grandma finally figured that out before she died. Let's not wait for another funeral for us to be together." The tears were starting to strain my throat. The last thing I said in my talk, squeaked, really, was, "We're the only family we have."

I burst into the tears that I had hoped were dried up and returned to my seat next to Mom. Nobody moved for several minutes as I sobbed. Then Jack stood and approached the podium.

"I've known Lorraine since Brandy was a teenager. Lorraine could be hard to get to know sometimes, and I often felt she was bitter about a lot of things. But I know that despite it all, she loved the people in this room. She could have been more open and loving, but she was a good person nonetheless."

He looked at me. "I am so happy Maureen was able to get to know the softer woman inside Lorraine, even if only for a short time." He smiled at me. "I think she took from those times a valuable lesson. If you love someone, show it while you can. Once they're gone, it's too late."

He took a deep breath and said, "Brandy told me she and Lorraine began talking for hours on the phone. I think despite their being unable to visit face-to-face that they were able to dwell in their love for each other—a love that had always been there but had grown dormant over time."

Looking at the urn, he said, "Goodbye, Lorraine. You kept your best lesson for us for the end. Thank you."

Jack nodded at someone in the back, and the man who had started the ceremony came forward and announced that the service was now over.

Jack said he had arranged for a boat to take us out into the Gulf, where we would scatter my grandmother's ashes.

As we walked out, Uncle Ryan and Mom talked for a bit. Then he looked at me and said, "It's settled. I'll be requesting a transfer back to the states. We'll begin seeing each other more often once that's done."

I smiled at him and said, "Thank you. I love you."

He smiled back. "I love you, too."

An hour later, we were floating on the Gulf of Mexico, its emerald waters stretching for miles in every direction.

Jack stepped forward and said, "When I was a boy and it would storm, I would float twigs on the road wash that led into gutters that emptied into the Gulf. I thought of the twigs as alive. I often wondered how many of the twigs made it to the Gulf to float on its vastness. I felt that was what they should be meant for—that life of freedom and possibility. Now, we are here to scatter Lorraine's ashes into that vastness. I hope the symbolic nature of floating on the Gulf inspires us all."

With that, he indicated for Mom, Uncle Ryan, and me to come forward. Opening the lid of the urn, he said, "Ashes to ashes, dust to dust. And to the world those ashes return."

We each reached in and grabbed a handful of Grandma's ashes and dropped them into the water. Others stepped forward and did the same, including Jack and Jenny. After that, Mom took the urn and turned it upside down over the waves. The remaining ashes scattered onto the surface, floating there for a moment before sinking.

Uncle Ryan took the urn and leaned over the railing of the boat, filling the urn with water and swishing it around before dumping it all back into the Gulf.

Before taking Mom back to the rehab center, we all gathered at Jack and Jenny's. We chatted and I did my best to get to know my cousins. I could tell they thought I was weird for saying what I did at the service, but I didn't care. I felt it needed to be said, and apparently, Uncle Ryan agreed. Before they left for their hotel, he thanked me and gave me a big hug.

"This won't be the last one, I hope," he said.

"It better not be," I answered.

36

That was three years ago. Like I said before, that feels like a week, and it feels like ten years. A lot has happened since then. For one thing, Mom let me get a dog. She's a mutt, but I love her. I named her Cleopatra because she thinks she rules the world, and maybe she does. Well, my world anyway.

Most of what has happened, though, is about Nick and his father's death. It turns out his bosses were running some kind of scheme that made them billions of dollars. It ended up in the news, and it felt weird to see a picture of Nick's dad on CNN and all the other networks. He's hailed as something of a hero for exposing their activities, but Nick said he'd prefer a living father to a dead hero. I don't blame him. I've never had one, and I sometimes wonder how different my life would be if I did.

The trial took place earlier this year, and the prosecutors got someone to turn against the guys running the whole thing. Jack said they'd probably get life in prison. They even arrested the guy who was hired to kill Nick's dad based on the information provided by the guy who turned against the others. The killer's trial won't be until next year maybe. Jack said the wheels of justice do more than turn slowly. He says they crawl like an hour hand.

Nick's family moved back to California. I miss

him, but we are able to call, text, and email each other. We're also friends on Facebook. I'm happy he has a normal life now, and he never thinks about killing himself anymore. He told me it feels weird that he ever did. He says he wants to eventually work with suicidal kids, so he's planning on getting his PhD in psychology one day.

Jenny and Jack are doing well, of course. I'm thinking of being a lawyer one day. Jack lets me come to court with him sometimes when he's defending someone. He told me that like most lawyers, most of his clients are guilty, but occasionally one isn't. At least they aren't guilty of the level of crime they're accused of, so he at least aims for a lesser charge. I guess you'd say he was the closest thing I have to a father. We're so close I call him Uncle Jack now. Jenny, who's like a second mom, is Aunt Jenny.

Mom came home, of course, and we moved back into our house. It felt weird not having Grandma there. Mom has a limp she'll have the rest of her life, and her left arm aches a lot of the time. She can't really lift anything heavy. She hired someone to manage the nursery business, and she only goes there for a couple of hours a day, so that's nice, though I'm sure she'd prefer to be working full time.

Uncle Ryan was given his transfer. He's stationed at MacDill Air Force Base in Tampa. We visit each other every six months, in December for Christmas and June right after school lets out. We alternate each year, with Mom and me traveling one year and Uncle Ryan's family the next. That way we each host Christmas every other year.

I've gotten to know my cousins a lot better now. They told me at first they were mad at me for what I said at Grandma's funeral, but now they're happy about it because they live near a beach and get to see us twice a year. Missing their friends in Germany is the worst part of being back in the states, but with all the ways people can keep up with each other, they still communicate with them.

Anyway, that's how it is now. Jack once told me either life goes on or it doesn't. He wasn't talking about dying. He was talking about what he calls *carpe diem*, or seize the day. He told me that while we might not be able to live life to its fullest every day, it shouldn't stop us from trying. He showed me a really old movie once called *Auntie Mame*. It was really funny, but like most great movies that are funny, it was also about serious things, like living life to its fullest, loving every minute of it, and being kind to people. I guess ultimately, it was about love and how happiness comes from attitude. That's my favorite movie now. I have it on DVD, which Jack and Jenny gave me for Christmas, and I watch it at least four times a year. It reminds me of what is now one of my favorite Dawsonisms: A life well lived is a life well loved.

It's August, and school starts in a few weeks. I'll be a sophomore. Sometimes, I wonder what adventures await me there. Then I wonder what adventures await me in college and in life. Some will be good. Some will be bad. But it's my life, and I intend to live it to the fullest.

If you or anyone you know is struggling with thoughts of suicide, please know there is help out there. The suicide hotline, a free service, can be reached by dialing 9-8-8. This new number went into effect in 2022. You and your life are important. Get help, please.

AFTERWORD

Thank you for reading my latest in the *Twigs* series. I like this one. It has the same feel to me that *Floating Twigs* has. I like Maureen. She's as complicated as anyone entering adolescence. She worries about things many adults would realize were not worth worrying about, but she learns from life as she moves through it.

I've been told by several readers that I write teenage characters well. That probably comes from teaching middle and high school English for three decades. I felt it was my job to learn what made my students "tick," as they say. What drove them? What was important to them? Many of my former students are still in touch through social media, and while I am proud of my work and success as an author, I am most proud of the positive influence I had on so many young lives.

If teen characters are easy for me, then I must confess that the character of Lorraine was the most difficult one to write. She is like so many of us who are well-meaning but fall short much of the time in our efforts to be pleasant. It was this dichotomy that made her both interesting and difficult to write. She is a good person who sometimes failed at being seen as good because of her past and her inability to let the past go. I believe 95% of the people in the world, like Lorraine, try to be a good person but often fall short of their own expectations for themselves. I consider that forgivable.

Finally, I must admit to having very little knowledge of accounting. I used this lack of knowledge to my benefit by choosing not to go into details about whatever the crucial documents in this book proved. If I've erred, forgive me. All I know is that a) people in illegal businesses often do keep private, accurate records of the money spent and earned while using "cleaned" books to share with the government, and b) it is possible for those records to be deciphered by a good accountant. That's what I know and what I used here. I think it worked fine for what I needed in the novel.

I have another Twigs book in mind, maybe two, so there will be another *Twigs* book that takes place in the small universe of Denton, Florida. It just needs to percolate once the idea forms beyond a thought. I expect the next one to come out in the summer of 2024.

My next novel will be the fourth in my Detective Tony Pantera series. I have many fans of that series as well, and the muses must be satisfied. I admit they are much darker and more difficult for some readers, but that's how crime fiction is. Crimes that hurt people on a personal level are very ugly, making the act of bringing the perpetrator to justice rewarding.

I am available for book club interviews either online through Zoom or in person. I do Zoom interviews for free, and will travel as long as the book club is able to provide me and possibly my wife with overnight accommodations. You can contact me by going to charlestabb.com.

Again, thank you. I would write books even if nobody read them, but it's nice that you do.

Made in the USA
Monee, IL
11 November 2024

69852817R10167